Mazy

And

The Cornish Pirates.

By Peter Price

CONTENTS

Yo, Ho, Ho and a saucer of milk………

FeeBe

Chapter one

Return of The Black Booger.

It was late evening in the port of Charlestown. The light was beginning to fade away into a foggy darkness over the harbour. Seagulls were squabbling over some scraps of fish. Rigging on the tall ships creaked and groaned and somewhere could be heard the sound of an accordion being played badly.

Mazy peered through the dark evening fog. Her long crumpled brown jacket sparkled with drops of foggy water. Along the bottom edge of her skirt was a dirty grey line from where it dragged along the ground. Pulled down over her ears was a red and white stripy woollen hat, which was wet through. She was waiting for the infamous pirate ship, The Black Booger, which was due back into port that evening. Her uncle, Blind

Lightning Henry, was the captain. Known throughout the waters of the Cornish coast as a fearsome Pirate, Blind Lightning Henry struck terror wherever he went. Mazy didn't believe a word of what she had heard about him. She knew him as someone who liked to make out he was a fearsome pirate by always shouting and telling tall stories about his adventures. Pirates, she thought, are supposed to have piles of treasure and gold coins. Her uncle never had any money and was always trying to borrow some to pay for his next Pirate expedition.

The most fantastic adventure story her uncle liked to repeat over and over again was the time he single-handedly fought a gigantic sea serpent during a mighty thunderstorm. All-day they fought as the thunder and lightning bounced off the huge waves. A bolt of lightning had crashed backwards and forwards between the masts of the ship and the exploding woodwork frightened the sea serpent away which dived back down into the boiling sea. Disastrously the lightning landed on top of her uncle's head, which had caused him to lose his hair and his eyesight. From that day on he was named Blind Lightning Henry. Although he could no longer see he reckoned he could tell which way to go by smelling the air. If it was salty he was facing the sea and if it wasn't then he was facing the land. His nose was so good he could tell the difference between gold and silver just by sniffing it.

On a later expedition, he acquired a colourful parrot and tried to train it to shout out 'Left a bit' and 'Right a bit' to guide him around the ship and when he was ashore. Unfortunately, the parrot never learnt to say more than, 'Left a bit'. As a result, her uncle had been pulled out of the harbour on several occasions when he should have turned right but followed the parrot's instruction, 'left a bit', and fell into the harbour instead. Mazy liked to hold her uncle's hand when he came ashore to make sure he didn't fall into trouble.

The Black Booger was due back that evening from another amazing expedition. Mazy wondered what it would be like to sail away from her home village. There were so many exciting places to go and visit. She so wanted to travel to the hot steamy jungle where her uncle had found 'Left a Bit' as his parrot was referred to. She would love to have a parrot to herself. She knew she could train it better than her uncle. She would teach it to say 'Right a bit' and with a parrot on each shoulder they could navigate her uncle around the harbour without him falling in.

She squinted through the swirling fog but it was the

slap of water and the low sounds of the crew that alerted her to the approach of her uncle's ship. She moved away from the shelter of the barrel as she saw the grey shape of a large, tall ship emerge from out of the fog.

It was The Black Booger.

She heard voices.

'Steady as she goes.'

'Slowly now boys.'

'Nearly there, jump ashore, Jory, and make fast.'

Mazy watched a young boy, slightly older than her, leap over the side of the ship and onto the harbour. He carried a coil of rope which he quickly tied through a metal ring attached to the ground. The Black Booger slowly came to a stop scraping alongside the harbour wall. The ship filled the whole of the remaining space as it was so large.

Mazy knew Jory was the newest member of The Black Booger's crew. He had been attending Mrs Scroggin's school, in a class above hers. He had been, but he had been summoned by her uncle to be the new ship's boy. Mrs Scroggin had screeched at the captain when he came to take the boy away to sea.

'He needs a heducation,' she screeched. 'Not some gallivanting, seafaring, waste of time.'

'He'll get a better education going to sea with me,' retorted Blind Lightning Henry. 'He hasn't learnt anything here,' as he grabbed Jory by the arm.

'Tish toss and throw a penny in the sea. What are you going to teach him? You aint even a proper Pirate what with all your fancy ways,' replied the schoolmistress wagging a long bony finger.

Mazy and all the other children in the school pressed their noses up against the windows and peered through the open classroom door. Listening to the two grownups having a shouty argument was the most exciting thing that had happened that year. The children were mostly afraid of Mrs Scroggin but they were all afraid of the most fearsome pirate in Cornwall, Blind Lightning Henry, all of them, excepting Mazy of course.

'I shall teach him to sail a ship across the mighty oceans,' boomed the Pirate Captain, 'to find his way by the stars and the sun and the moon and he will become a rich man in time.'

Mrs Scroggin shrieked with laughter and holding her

sides she shouted back, 'Rich? Rich? Why, Henry, 'I'm a fearsome Pirate', couldn't scrape more than two pence together the last time he came back. Had to borrow some money off your poor mother again to pay the crew.'

'Terrible storms we had,' said Henry as he grabbed hold of Jory and started dragging him out through the classroom door. 'Lost all our treasure overboard. Had to throw the rest away to stop us sinking.'

'Oh take him, you mad Pirate. Maybe he will be better off with you. Leastways you can educate him to spot a fool the next time one comes along.'

With that, the captain strode off down towards the harbour dragging Jory behind him. Mazy watched them go and wished she could have gone in Jory's place. She already knew her uncle was a fool but she really, really wanted to go to sea. And now, Jory had returned from his first trip. Mazy was consumed with curiosity. Her uncle was always full of fantastic tales, half of which she didn't believe and the other half she was sure he had made up. She wanted to know what really went on. Was there treasure, shipwrecks, mermaids, sea dragons or was it all just stories.

Mazy walked over to Jory, 'Exciting trip?' she asked looking up at the rigging and out to sea trying not to look too interested.

'Go away Mazy.'

Mazy pulled her wet woollen hat from her head and rung the foggy water out over Jory's shoes.

'Oi!' he shouted as Mazy ran away giggling.

'I'm going away now,' she shouted back at Jory as she

raced up the gangway and onto the deck of The Black Booger.

A familiar voice called out as she ran along the deck. 'Hello Mazy.'

She looked around to see Mr Fizz waving at her. Mr Fizz was the only crewman on the ship trusted to be in charge of the gunpowder. He was a short but round man with an enormous bushy beard. His legs were incredibly skinny and Mazy often wondered how he didn't fall over and roll around the deck like a giant bearded egg.

Mazy skidded to a stop alongside him, 'Hello Mr Fizz, glad to be back?'

'Glad as ever I shall be when alls been here and done.'

'What's left to do?' Mazy asked. 'Share out all the

treasure?'

Mr Fizz laughed, 'Treasure, now that would be a fine how did you do, wouldn't it now? You want to know how much treasure we be all a'getting you'd better get that question over to your uncle.'

Mazy turned and ran across the deck towards the captain's cabin. She threw open the door and exclaimed, 'Welcome back uncle.'

Left a bit shrieked, 'Left a bit,' flapping his wings and showering little green feathers everywhere. There was no one else in the cabin. Her uncle was nowhere to be seen.

'Hello left a bit,' said Mazy as she peered around the cabin. Mazy heard the sound of snoring from under the table. A long loud snore followed by two slightly shorter ones, a short silence and a long loud snore again.

Mazy bent down to look under the table and saw her uncle curled up on the floor, sucking his thumb and quite fast asleep. 'Uncle!' Mazy shouted and gave the sleeping figure a huge shove with her foot.

'What, what, what,' exclaimed her uncle. His eyes shot open wide and he sat up so quickly he banged his head on the underside of the table. He collapsed back down and tried to sit up again hitting his head a second time.

'We're under attack,' he shouted. 'Get down Mazy; I've been shot twice already.'

'Don't be silly, uncle,' said Mazy. 'You're home, tied up in port. Nearly all the crew have already gone ashore.'

'What? We're not under attack. I'm sure I heard gunfire.'

Mazy dragged on his arm, 'Come on uncle, get out from under the table,'

Blind Lightning Henry rolled over onto his knees, which wasn't that easy as the space under the table was quite small. 'Need to go on a diet,' he muttered as he finally rolled out across the cabin floor. He sat up and said, 'That you Mazy, good to hear your voice. Never thought I'd hear it again. Nearly been eaten by sharks on this trip.'

Mazy stared at him not believing what he was saying but wanting it to be true. She loved her uncle's stories. 'What happened?' she asked helping him to his feet.

'Treasure chest,' he replied. 'Finally found old Pirate

Pete's treasure chest. Had to fight off a hundred, no a thousand spiders before we could get our hands on it. Hauled it across to The Black Booger, on the skiff. Then the daft cook Gruntle, whose only job was to lift it onto the deck goes and slips it. Chest falls into the sea.'

'Oh no,' said Mazy did you lose it?'

'You know me Mazy. I'm not one to let go of a chest full of treasure. Dived straight in to recover it. Well, it had gone a long way down but I could see it lying on the sea bottom at a jaunty angle. Help me up girl.'

Mazy placed her arm around her uncle's shoulders and helped him to his feet. 'You actually came back with a chest full of treasure. I thought Mr Fizz was joking when he said to ask you about it.'

'Mr Fizz! Mr Fizz! Don't you go believing a word he

says. We didn't come back with any treasure.'

'Oh,' said Mazy. 'But I thought you swam down to recover it?'

'Oh I swam down alright,' continued her uncle as he buttoned up his blue and gold captain's jacket. 'But what I didn't see straight away were the sharks. Dozens, no hundreds of them. All circulating the chest and giving me the evil eye as if to say 'Come and take it if you dare.''

'So it's still down there,' said Mazy handing him his flintlock pistol and cutlass.

Her uncle thrust the pistol into the red waistband tied around his middle and attached his cutlass to his belt. 'Yes, it's still down there,' he continued. 'Not without a fight I might tell you. I biffed some sharks on their noses. Sharks don't like that. I grabbed two by their tails and tied them into a knot and then they all turned on me. I couldn't fight them all. See I couldn't hold my breath as long as they can. One of them bit off my leg before I gave up.'

Mazy glanced down at her uncle's two good legs. 'I'm still counting two good legs uncle.'

'You always were good at counting, Mazy. Now come on I've got an appointment at the Crab and Crossed Claws for a bowl of Mrs. Noggin's fish soup.' He crammed a black, three-pointed hat on top of his head and gathered up Left a Bit placing the parrot on his left shoulder. 'Right we're all set. Lead on Mazy.'

They left The Black Booger and made their way along the quay in the direction of the best place for food anywhere in Charlestown, The Crab and Crossed

Claws. 'Take my hand Mazy,' said her uncle as they walked off the gangplank. 'I know where I'm going but I would like to get there without falling into the harbour.'

Mazy slipped her hand into her uncle's hand and felt his huge rough fingers wrap themselves around hers. Her mind slipped back to the moment The Black Booger docked. 'How is Jory getting along?'

'Jory, he's a fine lad. Make a good sailor of him one day. Early days yet and he's a lot to learn but me and the crew will knock him into shape.'

'You won't be too hard on him, will you Uncle?'

'Can't be too hard on a new recruit, Mazy. They've got to learn how to take the knocks, make a man of him.'

'He is quite sensitive you know.'

'Sensitive!' roared her uncle. 'Oh my, wait until I tell him. Young Mazy thinks you're sensitive.'

'Please uncle don't you go saying any such thing or I'll push you in the harbour and tell everyone Left a Bit did it.'

'All right, Mazy, I won't go embarrassing the boy. But do I detect you have taken a bit of a shine to this handsome young sailor?'

Mazy felt a hot flush creep up her face. 'No, I do not,' she said.

Her uncle didn't say anything for a moment as they walked on in silence. Then he said, 'I may be blind but I can feel you blushing.'

'I am not blushing,' replied Mazy glad for once her uncle couldn't see her. 'What I am doing is wondering why you chose Jory in the first place. There are plenty of other young people you could have chosen.'

'It was Jory's mum and dad who asked me to take him,' answered her uncle. 'And it was Jory's idea. He was fed up trying to learn all that fancy stuff Mrs Scroggin tries to teach you. In any case, once the young lads have left school it's either fishing or mining and it all depends on whether you like being under the ground or on top of it. Jory didn't like the idea of being underground.'

Mazy steered her uncle around some handcarts which had been left out on the quay. She could see the yellow glow of lights shining out from the windows of The Crab and Crossed Claws. She knew once her uncle was there he would be too busy eating to talk to her anymore and she might never have the chance to ask him the question which had been building up inside her ever since she saw Jory head off out of the school.

'Uncle,' she started slowly, 'Why aren't there any girls onboard The Black Booger?'

Great Lightning Henry came to an abrupt stop as though he'd walked into a closed door.

'Girls?' he said. 'Well that's obvious. It's a well-known fact, girls on a ship bring nothing but bad luck. Very unlucky to have a girl on a ship. I thought everyone knew that.'

'But Mrs Scroggin goes out in a little boat and I've seen her daughter in a boat. Why isn't that unlucky?'

Her uncle snorted, 'That's boats, I'm talking about ships. No harm can come to anyone who's out in a boat but you need a powerful lot of good luck when you're sailing a ship. Whole different kettle of crustaceans.

No, I got nothing against women and boats but a female on The Black Booger would bring bad luck. None of my crew would sail with them anyway.'

'So you don't think losing a chest of gold over the side and losing one of your legs to a shark isn't bad luck.' said Mazy somewhat rudely.

Her uncle didn't seem to notice her change of tone. 'Well,' he said, drawing himself up to his full height to emphasise his next point. 'Well Mazy, think what would have become of us if there had been a woman on board? Would have lost both legs and The Black Booger. Nope, no women on my ship whilst I'm the captain and the last time I checked I am the captain of The Black Booger.'

Mazy and her uncle continued towards The Crab and Crossed Claws. Mazy saw the front door open and warm yellow light spill out onto the ground. She smelt hot fish soup and smelly sailors and sighed to herself. Not just unlucky she thought, wrinkling her nose. She didn't like fish soup and she didn't like the smell of unwashed pirates. She was never going to have an exciting adventure.

'Here we are uncle,' she said despondently.

'Thank you Mazy. You're the kindest girl I know. Anything I can do for you just you ask.'

'There is one thing uncle,' said Mazy, her hopes suddenly rising. 'Could you take me with you on your next adventure? I'd be very good and I'd obey all the orders and I'm sure I wouldn't bring any bad luck. And all the crew know me I'm sure they would still sail with you. I only take up a little space and I'm not very heavy and I know how to cook so I could help Gruntle with the cooking.' Mazy could hardly say the words fast enough as she spelt out her whole desire to go to sea in The Black Booger.

Her uncle paused at the doorway into The Crab and Crossed Claws. He frowned down at Mazy and he suddenly looked very stern. 'You tried to trick me Mazy what with all that talk of girls on my ship. You was just leading me to this question. I don't like the way you did that but I'll forgive you this once for your help this evening. I did say I would do anything but that is not something I can do. I told you, no women or foolish young girls will ever travel on The Black Booger. You're bad luck. All of you,' and with that he strode into The Crab and Crossed Claws and the door slammed shut in Mazy's face.

Chapter Two

FeeBe and Mrs. Scroggin.

Mazy turned her back on The Crab and Crossed Claws.
Her teeth chattered as she walked up the cobbled path
towards her home. She shivered and held her arms
tightly around her waist. All the time she had been
waiting for The Black Booger to arrive the cold damp
fog had squeezed its way right inside her long coat.
Water dripped off the end of her nose as she bent down
to find the back door key under the flowerpot.

'Is that you Mazy?' she heard her mum call out.

'Yes, mum, it's me.'

Mazy hung up her soaking wet coat on a hook by the
back door and walked into the small kitchen where
there was a hot stove keeping the cottage all warm and

cosy. Her mum was sat in a rocking chair mending an old sock. 'You're out late tonight,' she said.

Mazy sat down as close as she could to the stove without actually burning herself. She drew her knees up to her chest and wrapped her arms around them.

'I've been waiting for The Black Booger,'

'And did it come in?'

'Yes, it came.'

Mazy didn't say any more, she was still thinking about her uncle's stern look at the door of The Crab and Crossed Claws. She hadn't meant to upset him but he did offer. It was so unfair. 'Am I bad luck?' she said looking up at her mum who was cutting off the darning thread from the repaired sock.

'Bad luck? What a funny question. Course you aren't

Mazy love. Who's been telling you such daft tales like that?'

'Uncle Henry, he says girls are bad luck.'

'Your Uncle Henry doesn't know a thing. He's been at sea for so long he's got seawater for brains. Sloshing about like water in a bucket. I swear you can hear it when he's walking along. You don't want to worry your head about a daft old pirate like him.'

Her mum stood up and arranged the sock with some others over the stove. 'There, your dad will have a nice pair of nearly new, warm socks tomorrow.'

'Where's dad going?'

'He's managed to persuade Thomas to let him help with the lobster pots. Hopefully, if there are enough of them filled it may mean a bit more work. Goodness knows we could do with the money.'

Mazy's dad didn't have a regular job any more. He used to mend the fishing boats when they had been damaged on the rocks or in storms. But last year there had been a terrible accident at the boatyard and her dad had been crushed by a boat which had toppled over. It took a long time for him to heal up and he'd lost all his strength. There was little work in the harbour for him to earn some money. Mazy knew they didn't have very much money and so she never asked for anything.

It was so annoying she couldn't join Jory and the rest of the crew on The Black Booger. She would have made sure the treasure chest had been tied up before it was lifted onto the boat; then it wouldn't have fallen back into the sea. They would have all been rich and her dad wouldn't have to look for work. How could her uncle have been so stupid?

Her mum opened a drawer and put away the darning. 'There's a hot potato on the stove keeping warm for you if you like,'

Mazy's stomach gurgled at the thought of some hot food. 'Thanks mum,' she replied.

'I also kept a little milk back for FeeBe. It's on the table. I'm off to my bed now. Don't you be late neither; you've got school in the morning.'

'Yes mum,' mumbled Mazy, her mouth full of hot potato. When she had finished eating she poured the milk, her mum had left out, into a saucer and placed it on the floor.

'FeeBe,' she called.

A small black cat uncurled itself from under the table

and stretched out its back. FeeBe was Mazy's cat but her mum looked after it most of the time. The cat walked delicately over to Mazy and closing its eyes lapped at the milk in the saucer. Mazy gently stroked the cat's back and heard it purring loudly as it drank the milk.

FeeBe had been a tiny, bedraggled, wet kitten when Mazy found it behind the woodshed.

'Been abandoned by its mother,' her mum had said when Mazy brought the tiny bundle of wet fur into the cottage. 'What do you intend doing with it?'

'I'm going to keep it,' said Mazy.

'Oh good,' complained her dad, 'another mouth to feed, just what we need.'

'Don't you go taking any notice of him,' said her mum

peering down at the little kitten. 'I'm sure we can accommodate a little creature like that.'

'Thanks mum,' said Mazy. 'I promise I'll look after her.'

Her dad came to look at the kitten, 'Look at her; she's already got Feed Me written all over her.'

'Oh go away and let the girl have something to herself,' said mum pushing him out of the way. 'What are you going to call her Mazy? She's got to have a name.'

Mazy thought for a moment, 'FeeBe. That will always remind me I have to feed her.'

Once FeeBe had finished her milk she climbed into Mazy's lap. 'We're not unlucky are we FeeBe?' Mazy said, stroking the cat. 'It was lucky for you I found you and lucky for me finding you.' Mazy could feel

FeeBe's body vibrating as the cat purred. Mazy's eyes closed and for a moment she dozed off in front of the warm stove. 'Oh my,' she said, waking up suddenly. 'I must go to bed or I will sleep with you all night.'

'Good night FeeBe,' yawned Mazy and she tipped the cat off her lap and made her way up to bed.

The following morning Mazy was up with the sunrise. It was a school day so she grabbed her books and ran down the path towards the harbour. Running in the same direction was her best friend, Melwyn.

'Hi Smelly Mellie,' called out Mazy as she caught up with her friend.

'Hi Crazy Mazy,' replied Melwyn. 'I see The Black Booger is back. Have you seen your uncle yet?'

'Saw him last night going to The Crab and Crossed

Claws. They found a treasure chest and they lost it in shark-infested water and uncle tried to get it back and was nearly eaten by one of the sharks. It sounded really exciting,' said Mazy breathlessly, as the two girls continued running towards the schoolhouse.

'Your uncle's crazy,' panted Melwyn. 'Was Jory there?'

'I saw him but he told me to go away.'

'He likes you then.'

'He does not; he was so rude to me.'

'When boys are rude to you and tell you to go away it means they like you.'

'You're crazy. Anyway, old Mr. Massen told me to go away and he definitely doesn't like me.'

'He told you to go away because you was in his field stealing his apples.'

'I was not so,' replied Mazy pushing her friend sideways. 'I wasn't stealing them apples I was liberating them from the clutches of the evil apple tree. The tree hangs on to them until they go bad. So I helped some escape.'

'So you could eat them.'

'Maybe I did, maybe I didn't.'

They slowed down to a walk as the pathway began to climb up towards the granite schoolhouse.

'Did you ask your uncle if you could go sailing away with him?' asked Melwyn.

'I did,' replied Mazy sourly.

'He said no didn't he?'

'He did,' said Mazy.

'Why won't he take you?'

Mazy stopped at the steps leading up to the open school door and turned to her friend, ''Cos he's an arrogant, stuck up, stupid old man who thinks he's a pirate but he isn't really.'

'That is no way to speak, Miss Mazy Ansell,' boomed a screechy voice, from the entrance to the school. Mazy turned around and saw her school teacher, Mrs Scroggin, glaring at her.

'Sorry, Mrs Scroggin,' said Mazy trying to sound like she was apologising when she wasn't.

'And to whom were your rude words directed?' inquired Mrs Scroggin.

'She was talking about her uncle, Blind Lightning Henry, Miss,' said Melwyn helpfully.

'What! That pompous old fool? That stupid man who thinks he can just waltz in here and take one of my best students and teach him how not to be a pirate. Man's an idiot. Don't you go having anything to do with him. That goes for you too Mazy Ansell,' finished Mrs Scroggin as she swirled around and returned inside.

Mazy and Melwyn grinned at each other and joined the other children who were all jostling through the school doorway.

Mazy took her seat by the window and looked down over Charlestown Harbour. She could see the local fishermen setting up sails, hauling on ropes, and gathering up the nets which they used for fishing. The harbour was a hive of activity as the tide was on the turn. The boats, some small and some quite large began to move slowly from their moorings; manoeuvring around each other and setting off out to sea. Mazy thought she saw her dad on one of the smaller crabbing boats. She hoped he had a good day. The noisy seagulls followed the fishing boats hoping for some odd scraps of fish to be thrown their way. Boats went off in all directions. The crabbing boats headed out to where they had placed their crab pots. The fishing boats heading further out to sea to favourite places where each captain hoped he would make a good catch of fish. Until the last vessel left in the harbour was The Black Booger.

Mazy stared at her uncle's ship wondering when it too would set sail. The Black Booger was indeed all black. The hull of the ship was black, the decks were painted black and the masts were painted black. Black sails hung from the masts. 'At night,' her uncle had said, 'we can sneak up on the enemy without them seeing us.'

'Who are the enemy?' Mazy had asked and her uncle told her one of his stories.

'Anybody with a cargo of gold and diamonds and rubies and pearls. We sneak up, overpower the ship's crew and steal all their treasure. We've taken ships twice the size, no five times the size as The Black Booger, but they didn't see us in the dark. Fearsome battles we had. Fighting them hand to hand in the darkness. They didn't know who was who, it was so dark. And we rubbed coal on our faces so we were all black too. If we couldn't see someone we knew it was one of us.'

'But what do you do with all the treasure?' asked Mazy.

'I've never seen any and you've never got any money.'

'Buried,' whispered her uncle in a loud whisper as if someone was listening and couldn't quite hear. 'Buried on a secret island under some palm trees. Can't be bringing it home. Someone might rob me of it.'

When her uncle told such incredible stories they always seemed so true to Mazy. But sat in school and looking at The Black Booger, all tied up, they started to seem nothing more than just stories.

Mazy sighed. She would love to be on one of her uncle's adventures, although she wasn't sure she would like to be involved in a fight; treasure or no treasure.

A figure caught her eye and she saw Jory leave the ship. He was walking up the hill in the direction of the school. He had changed somehow. He looked taller and more suntanned. She was sorry she had rung out her hat on his feet. She wanted to talk to him and to find out where he had been and what he had seen on his first voyage.

'I'll thank you to look at the board and not the boy,' Mrs Scroggin said in a loud voice behind Mazy's desk.

'I was just looking at the boats, Mrs Scroggin.' replied Mazy.

Mrs Scroggin bent over and looked out of the window. 'Who is that walking up the hill towards us?' she asked Mazy.

'It's Jory, Mrs Scroggin.'

'And is he a boy or a girl?'

'He's a boy.'

'Exactly so. He's a boy.'

Mrs Scroggin straightened up. 'As I said your eyes on the board, not on the boy.'

'Yes, Mrs Scroggin.'

Several of the other children in the class sniggered but Mazy ignored them. She sneaked another look out of the window behind Mrs Scroggin's back but Jory had disappeared somewhere out of sight.

Chapter Three

Mazy gets into trouble.

In the lunch break, Mazy and Melwyn sat outside in the bright sunshine overlooking the harbour. 'Look,' said Melwyn, 'there's Jory. It looks like he's going back to your uncle's ship.'

Mazy shielded her eyes from the sun and watched Jory striding down the path towards the harbour.

'I wonder where he's been,' she said.

'He's got an aunty up above the schoolhouse, in one of the old cottages. I 'spect he's been there for his lunch.'

Mazy stood up, 'I'm going to go and see him.'

'You can't go now,' said Melwyn. 'You'll be late back for school.'

'Don't care,' replied Mazy. 'I want to find out what they all get up to when they go pirating. There's only one way to find out the truth and that's down there.'

'You're crazy Mazy.'

'That's me,' said Mazy as she left her friend and made her way towards the harbour and Jory who she knew was on The Back Booger.

When she arrived the ship was quiet. Mazy hadn't seen anyone onboard other than Jory. She presumed he had been left in charge as he was the youngest and newest of the crew. Normally she would have walked straight onto the ship but she paused. What if Jory was still angry with her? What if he thought she was a thief and he attacked her? Mazy's heart beat a little faster. 'Hello,' she tried to say but her mouth was dry and all that came out was a croak. Swallowing hard she tried again, 'Hello.'

There was no reply.

There was nothing for it but to go onboard and hope she could attract Jory's attention from the deck. She walked up the gangplank and onto the deck.

'Hello?' she tried again.

There was no reply.

'Is there anyone there?'

There was no reply.

Mazy crept forward to the stairs which led down inside the ship. Why am I creeping she thought. This is my uncle's ship. I am allowed on it whenever I like. She peered down into the darkness of the stairs.

'Hello?' she tried again.

There was no reply.

Her heart was beating hard in her chest as she slowly descended the stairs into the darkness below. 'Is there someone there?'

The ship was completely quiet. She arrived at the bottom of the stairs and paused to allow her eyesight to become accustomed to the darkness. She heard a hollow scraping noise. She squinted trying to see what could be making the noise. Was it a rat? All ships had rats. Mazy didn't mind rats, but you had to make sure you didn't step on one because it would bite you.

'Are you a rat?' she asked the darkness.

'No,' exclaimed a loud voice just behind her. 'I'm a big bad pirate.'

Mazy shrieked in surprise but when she spun around

she saw it was Jory, laughing at her.

'You horrible boy, scaring me like that.'

'Oh come on Mazy, it was just a bit of fun.'

'Fun for you, not for me. I thought I was going to die of shock.'

'Well, you frightened me too, creeping about.'

'Don't you try and blame me for anything Jory. I called out. You knew it was me.'

'What are you doing here anyway,' said Jory changing the subject. He hadn't meant to scare Mazy. Just make her jump a little and now she was mad at him.

'I came to see you but I don't know why I bothered. You're such a stupid, annoying person.' Mazy started to climb back up the stairs to the ship's deck when Jory called her back.

'Don't go Mazy, I'm sorry I scared you. It's just that it's so boring being left on the ship all on my own.'

'Oh, poor Jory. All alone.'

'Don't Mazy, I said I'm sorry. Let's be friends again and I'll tell you all about being on your uncle's ship if you like. I know you're dying to know.'

Mazy turned around on the stairs and looked down at Jory. 'Well, I suppose I could give you five minutes of my time to listen to your tales.'

'Come on,' said Jory. 'Let's go to your uncle's cabin. He's not here and there's more room to sit and talk. If you like I can show you some of your uncle's treasure.'

Mazy stared at Jory. Was he telling the truth? Would she finally see some of the pirate treasure? All at once, she forgot he had scared her. She followed Jory as he led her below decks. They scrambled over boxes and barrels, past cannons and piles of rope, dodging under hammocks, finally to enter her uncle's cabin.

The last time she was in here her uncle was asleep under the table. 'Are you allowed in here?' she asked Jory. She didn't want him in trouble on her behalf.

'Oh yeah, I'm in charge of the ship so I can go anywhere I like.'

Mazy examined her uncle's cabin properly for the first time. Normally she just met him and they left as soon as she arrived. In the centre of the cabin was the round oak table under which Mazy had earlier found her uncle asleep. The tabletop was smooth but had some faint carved letters around the edge. She leant across and read the words out loud.

'This table belongs to Captain Jehoshaphat the Terrible. A curse on anyone who eats off it.'

She looked up at Jory who was grinning at her. 'Who is Captain Jehoshaphat?' she asked, 'and why was he so terrible?'

'He was your uncle's best friend from years ago. They sailed together on this ship, although it wasn't called The Black Booger then.'

Mazy suddenly had a million questions but started with, 'What was it called?'

'The Scarlet Arrow.'

'The Scarlet Arrow,' repeated Mazy, 'what a lovely name. But what happened to Jehoshaphat and why is the ship now called The Black Booger and why is the table cursed and when will I see some treasure?'

'Oh Mazy,' laughed Jory. 'You're full of questions. One at a time, please. Which one should I answer first?'

'Um,' Mazy thought for a moment. 'What happened to my uncle's friend? Is he still alive?'

'That I don't know. I didn't know much about your uncle before I came on board and I've only been on one trip so far.'

'So which question can I ask that you know the answer to?' said Mazy crossly. She had been hoping Jory would tell her an exciting story about pirates and curses but he didn't know anything.

'How about I show you some treasure your uncle keeps, I think he took it from Jehoshaphat but I'm not sure. He keeps it locked in a chest under his bed.'

Jory squeezed around the edge of the table, ducked

under a low wooden beam and knelt on the floor. Mazy

watched him reach under the small cot bed and drag out

a wooden box. Her heart was pumping hard in her

chest. How much treasure could there be she

wondered? It was a small box but it might be a huge

diamond or ruby. Mazy leant forward to look over

Jory's shoulder when she heard the thump of footsteps

on the deck above. Jory turned his head and looked up

towards the sound. He froze, his eyes wide open.

The footsteps could be heard descending the steps.

Jory thrust the chest back under the bed. He shot up and

as the cabin door began to open he shouted 'What are

you doing in here?'

Mazy looked at him astonished. 'You're not supposed

to be in here,' he continued in a loud voice as the cabin

door opened to reveal Mazy's uncle, Blind Lightning

Henry.

'What is the meaning of this?' roared Blind Lightning Henry. He might have been blind but he always seemed to know who was in front of him.

'Left a bit,' screamed Left a Bit, violently flapping its wings.

'Be quiet you stupid parrot,' said the captain and placed the bird on its perch.

'Well? the captain continued.

Before Mazy could say anything she heard Jory say, 'Begging you pardon captain. Junior Seaman Jory, reporting. I was on watch when I heard a suspicious noise coming from your cabin. When I came to investigate I found your niece Mazy skulking about. I was about to escort her ashore.'

'Mazy is that you?'

'Yes uncle, but it wasn't like that at all, Jory….' But before she could continue Jory cut across her. 'I know you don't like girls onboard Captain, They are bad luck so I was hoping to escort her off before you arrived. I am sorry I failed in that duty.'

'Failed in that duty?' exclaimed Mazy, not believing her ears. 'But uncle.'

'Not another word Mazy,' interrupted her uncle. 'You know I don't have girls onboard. Young Jory's quite right. You're all bad luck. Jory, escort the trespasser off the ship. And Mazy, I'd thank you never to return.'

Mazy was too stunned by what had happened to reply. She felt tears beginning to well up in her eyes as she turned around and made her way up the stairs to the top deck of the ship. She heard her uncle behind her praising Jory. 'Well done my lad. Glad to see you're alert on watch. Just what we need. Trespassers, just what we don't need. Specially female ones.'

Mazy's heart felt like a lead weight inside her chest. She dragged her sleeve across her face to wipe away the tears in her eyes. She hated it when she cried. How could Jory be so mean and tell so many lies? She thought they were friends. 'I hate him,' she whispered loudly to herself. She looked out across the harbour and saw some of the other crew heading back towards the ship. She sprinted down the gangplank and turned towards the beach.

.

Chapter Four

Storm.

'I don't know, Mrs Scroggin', said Melwyn. 'I just know she said she didn't feel well and had to go home.'

Mrs Scroggin stared hard at Melwyn. Mazy's absence from school hadn't gone unnoticed and Mrs Scroggin didn't believe for one moment that Mazy had gone home, sick. Melwyn stared back trying her best to look innocent.

'Well,' said Mrs Scroggin finally, 'I shall hope Miss Mazy will bless us with her company tomorrow morning. You may tell your friend I shall expect nothing more than a written note from her mother explaining the symptoms of her illness and what has been done to prevent a re-occurrence.'

'Yes Mrs Scroggin,' replied Melwyn feeling a little relieved. She knew, as did Mrs Scroggin, that Mazy's mum couldn't read or write.

Time passed slowly and Melwyn thought the bell to end school would never come. When it finally rang Melwyn ran out of the school, down the path and towards the harbour to look for Mazy. Melwyn searched around the harbour. She looked into the smaller boats tied up and across the deck of The Black Booger but Mazy was nowhere to be seen. Two fishermen were unloading fish from their boat so she asked them if they had seen Mazy anywhere.

'Down on the beach,' one replied. 'She's sitting behind a great big rock near the edge of the sea. You'd better warn her not to get washed away.'

'Thanks,' called Melwyn as she ran off towards the

seashore and the big rock.

Behind the big rock, she found her friend, sat with her arms wrapped around her knees and staring out to sea.

'You all right?' she asked sitting down next to Mazy.

'No I am not,' muttered Mazy.

'Didn't get to see your boyfriend then?' asked Melwyn.

'He is not my boyfriend,' shouted Mazy, standing up as she did so. She kicked a stone far out into the sea. 'He's a stuck up, lying, no good, stupid idiot who's not fit to be a pirate or a friend or, or, or, anything.'

Melwyn decided it would be safer not to say anything as she could see how angry Mazy was. She looked up at her friend who was frowning hard and staring out to sea. Eventually Mazy dropped down beside her. 'I'm sorry I shouted,' said Mazy, 'but it was going really well. Jory was going to show me some of my uncle's treasure. But when uncle came back to the ship Jory made out I was trespassing and he'd caught me. Now I'm not allowed on the ship at all.'

'Why did he do that?' asked Melwyn.

'I don't know. I don't think we were supposed to be in the Captain's cabin and I'm certain we shouldn't have been looking in the treasure chest.'

'I suppose Jory didn't want to get into trouble.'

'But why did he get me into trouble?' Mazy picked up a stone and threw it as hard as she could into the sea. Melwyn looked down at the beach and picked up a round pebble. She threw hers as far as she could. The splash was further out to sea than the one left by Mazy's stone.

'You throw like a shifty little boy called Jory,' laughed Melwyn.

'I do not,' replied Mazy. She picked up another stone and threw it as hard as she could. The splash appeared a long way out, frightening a lone seagull.

'Mrs Scroggin wants a note from your mum,' said Melwyn as she threw another stone.

'Mrs Scroggin knows my mum can't write, why'd she say that?'

'I think it was to frighten the younger kids in case they thought of going sick.'

'I hate Mrs Scroggin,' shouted Mazy and threw another stone. 'And I hate school, and I hate Jory and I hate my uncle. Come on Melwyn, let's go and see what's for tea.'

The two girls walked slowly off the beach and up towards the harbour.

Mazy and Melwyn were so deep in conversation they didn't see Mr Borlaise who was sitting on a wooden bench outside The Crab and Crossed Claws. Mr Borlaise was the oldest man living in the village. He had a big white beard and sparkling blue eyes under his big bushy eyebrows. Mr Borlaise knew everybody and he knew everything that was going on. He looked up at the two girls as they walked past and said, 'Hello Miss Mazy and Miss Melwyn. Going home before the storm?'

'Oh hello Mr. Borlaise,' said Mazy, 'didn't see you there hiding under your eyebrows.'

Melwyn giggled nervously. 'Don't be so rude.'

'Don't you worry Miss Melwyn,' replied Mr. Borlaise, taking off his blue hat and scratching the top of his head. 'I might have bushy eyebrows but I don't miss seeing what's going on' He put his hat back on his head and looked at Mazy, 'How's your friend Jory keeping?'

'Oh well enough,' replied Mazy trying to avoid catching Mr. Borlaise in the eye but at the same time wondering what he might know. 'I haven't seen him since he became a pirate on my uncle's ship.'

Mr. Borlaise suddenly gave off a loud sneeze. 'Sorry,' he said, wiping his nose across the back of his sleeve. 'It's just that I'm allergic to people telling fancy stories.'

'You don't think he's a pirate?'

'Pirates? Overgrown schoolboys the lot of them. None

of them are real pirates. I reckon if they ever did meet a real pirate they'd run a mile. Or maybe sail a mile.'

'Well, what do they do when they leave here?'

'Good question,' said Mr. Borlaise. 'That I don't know but have you ever seen them bring back some treasure? That's what pirates are in it for, isn't it? Never seen so much as a gold coin.'

'Jory says uncle's got a treasure chest in his cabin.' said Mazy defensively.

'This the same Jory you haven't seen since he joined The Black Booger?'

Mazy stared at Mr. Borlaise realising he had caught her in a lie about not seeing Jory. Mr. Borlaise stared back at her his blues eyes twinkling with amusement.

Mazy finally shrugged her shoulders, 'I must have

heard it somewhere.'

'I guess you must have,' replied Mr. Borlaise.

'You said something about a storm?' interrupted Melwyn.

'That's right Miss Melwyn. Pressure's dropping and the wind has changed around the compass and the seagulls have flown inland. All the signs are there's a black storm a-coming. I suggest you two be safe at home before it arrives.'

'Thank you Mr. Borlaise,' said Melwyn. She grabbed Mazy by the arm and the two of them walked off the harbour and towards the safety of their homes.

The storm hit the coast just after dark. Jory was below decks on The Black Booger and heard the rain rattle across the deck and the wind snatching at the rigging. He was lying on a rolled-up sail in the sail locker and thinking about Mazy. Why was she so angry he wondered? Didn't she see he had to pretend to have caught her otherwise he would have been in so much trouble? They would have both been in trouble if her uncle had caught them. I did her a favour he thought and she got angry instead of going along with it.

Jory rolled backwards and forwards on the lumpy sail until he saw the face of Mr Fizz looking at him through the doorway of the sail locker.

'What?' said Jory grumpily.

'The cap'n wants all hands on deck to tighten up the rigging and tie down the hatches before the storm hits us. So get your happy face on and look lively.'

Jory rolled off the sail and followed Mr Fizz up to the top deck. The wind was coming in great gusts and the rain stung his face. Jory grabbed the side rail to steady himself. He wiped the water out of his eyes and went to help lock down the hatches on the deck. Rainwater ran down the back of his neck and soaked right through to the top of his trousers. Huge puddles began to form and the sailors splashed through them as they tied up ropes and gathered in anything that was lying loose. Blind Lightning Henry stood on the top deck shouting instructions but no one could hear a word he was saying above the noise of the wind and rain. A crack of lightning made Jory jump. He heard a long low rumble of thunder not far away. Mr Fizz was waving his arms and beckoning Jory to come back below decks. Jory splashed his way across the slippery deck when he saw a small black cat hiding under a ledge. The cat was soaked through and didn't have any protection from the weather. Jory changed direction towards the cat. He heard Mr Fizz call out his name. He looked across to where Mr Fizz was stood in the doorway and waved at him. 'In a minute,' he shouted. He didn't know if Mr Fizz had heard him but Jory was determined not to leave the cat outside in the storm. He bent down and lifted a wet and frightened cat and tucked it inside his shirt. Only then did he run to the open doorway where Mr Fizz was waiting for him.

'What you been doing?' asked Mr Fizz. 'I was shouting at you to get back inside.'

'There was a cat.'

'Cat? What are talking about?'

The small black cat poked its head out from Jory's shirt

and gave a little meow.

'You found a cat,' said Mr Fizz. 'Well good for you.'
And he turned around and clumped noisily down the
steps to the lower deck.

Jory carried the cat down below decks and made his
way to the galley. The Black Booger was rocking
slightly and Jory could feel the wind whistling through
the open decks. Each time the thunder boomed outside
the cat would give a little mewing sound. 'It's ok,' Jory
stroked the cat's head. 'Let's see if we can find you
some food and get you warm and dry.'

The galley was where the cook prepared the food. The
cook's name was Gruntle. He was a short fat man with
curly ginger hair; he had a round red face and was
always smiling. When Jory entered the galley he saw
Gruntle stirring a large pot of stew over a fire. 'Hello

Mr Jory, what have you got there?' said Gruntle looking up from the stew.

'I've rescued a cat from the weather. I found it on the deck soaked through so I've brought it in from the storm. I thought it might be able to dry out in front of the fire.'

Gruntle swapped his hands over but continued stirring his pot. He waved Jory towards the side of the galley. 'If you sit in there, you can both get warm and dry without getting too close to the fire.'

'Thanks,' said Jory gratefully. 'I don't suppose you have anything I can give the cat. I think it might be hungry.'

Gruntle pointed to a small barrel. 'Have a look in there, Jory. I can't leave off stirring. You may find some dried fish and there's some milk behind me on the shelf.'

Gruntle swapped hands again and wiped the sweat from his face. 'Hot in here,' he said as he watched Jory find a piece of fish. Jory put the fish down on the deck and put the cat next to it. He poured some milk out into a dish and placed it down in front of the cat too. Gruntle peered around the side of the pot and watched the cat eating the fish. 'Nice looking cat,' he said. 'Daresay someone will be looking for it later on.'

Jory looked up and frowned. 'You think it's somebody's cat?'

'Well, he's well-fed so someone's looking after him. Unless, of course, he's just a stray one and been taking care of himself.' Gruntle added quickly seeing the look on Jory's face.

'I rescued him so he's my cat now,' said Jory fiercely.

'You say so,' replied Gruntle who didn't care about cats. He was more interested in cooking. 'You going to give him a name?'

'Storm, I shall call him Storm.'

'Well, that's original. You didn't think of something more like Tiddles or Kitty?'

'Tiddles isn't very original. No, I found him in a storm so I will call him Storm.'

'Storm it is.' agreed Gruntle 'Now shift yourself, the crew will be joining us for dinner.'

Chapter Five

The Treasure Map.

Jory picked up Storm and cradling the cat in his arms he moved to the back of the galley and perched himself on top of one of the barrels. Mr Fizz, the gunpowder man, was the first one in followed by Sam and his brother Dave. Skirtle, who was good at mending the sails, sat down on one of the barrels and finally Mr Lost, who was the ship's navigator. They had their wooden bowls filled with Gruntle's hot stew and sat wherever there was a space.

'Wot you got there Jory?' asked Skirtle peering at the front of Jory's shirt. Skirtle was a bit short-sighted.

'It's a cat,' replied Jory stroking the top of Storms head.

'Ah,' said Skirtle, 'I thought it was some black goo

coming out your chest. Thought I might have to sew you up.'

There was little conversation as the crew were more interested in their stew.

'Nice stew,' mumbled Sam through the spoon in his mouth.

'Thanks,' replied Gruntle. 'Amazing what you can do with some turnips and stuff.'

You couldn't exactly say silence followed as there was a good deal of slurping and sucking on spoons. But what silence there might have been was rudely interrupted by Blind Lightning Henry bursting through the galley door. He was carrying a rolled-up map under one arm and his cutlass under the other. His eyes were wide, his face was red and he was panting. Left a Bit was clinging onto his shoulder.

'Soup?' ventured Gruntle offering a bowl.

'Soup? Soup?' shouted Blind Lightning Henry, 'No time for soup. Clear away that bench there.'

Sam and Dave stood up and pressed themselves against the side of the ship as Blind Lightning Henry unrolled his map and spread it out along the bench.

'Just got hold of this,' he wheezed. 'Took some doing. Gentleman who had it didn't want to let go of it. Had to fight him and his two, no five friends, but I still got it. Look!'

Fascinated, Jory and the rest of the crew leant forward to look at the captain's latest map. It showed an island with palm trees and lakes and forests and wild animals. It had illustrations of whales and large fishes swimming

Mazy and the Cornish Pirates

in the sea. It wasn't a bit like the usual navigation maps Mr Lost used.

'Where's that?' asked Dave.

'Can't tell you that yet. Only Mr Lost needs to know. But what I can tell you is this map is going to make us rich.' Blind Lightning Henry looked around the galley beaming with excitement.

Jory frowned. Something wasn't quite right and he couldn't quite work out what that something was. He looked at the map and at the captain and back at the map. The map was badly drawn and it could have been anywhere; so why was Blind Lightning Henry so excited.

Just a minute.

78

That's what's wrong.

Blind Lightning Henry was studying the map.

'Is the captain really blind?' whispered Jory in Sam's ear. Sam half turned his head towards Jory and whispered out of the corner of his mouth, 'If you value your life, then he's as blind as a bat from being hit by lightning.' Sam looked sideways at Jory and added, 'Do you value your life?'

Jory nodded his head vigorously. 'Blind as a bat,' he whispered back.

'No whispering at the back,' shouted (Not so) Blind

Lightning Henry.

All the crew went quiet waiting for the captain to explain the map. Mr Lost, the ship's navigator, leant forward and looked over Blind Lightning Henry's shoulder. 'Er captain,' he began cautiously, 'if you want me to navigate to that island I'm going to need some better information. Like where it is would be helpful.'

'Soon enough Mr Lost, soon enough. For now, this has to be a secret only I know 'cos this is the treasure map of that infamous pirate Davy Dreadlocks. This island here,' the Captain pointed to the map with a flourish of his hand, 'is where he buried his ill-gotten gains from pirating the seas around here.'

All the crew leant forward again, to look closely at this remarkable treasure map. Jory thought to himself if the captain had fought off five men to get hold of the map at least five other men knew where the treasure was hidden. But the excitement in the galley was so intense Jory quickly forgot about other men and began to imagine returning to Charlestown a rich man. Mazy would be so impressed she'd be his friend for life. I would let her have some small treasure for herself. His thoughts were interrupted by Mr Fizz saying, 'I hope this map's better'n the last one you had, begging your pardon Captain.'

The crew looked expectantly at Blind Lightning Henry.

'Nothing wrong with that map just that it wasn't by a well-known pirate. This one is. Got his signature.' Blind Lightning Henry held up the map for everyone to see. He pointed to the corner. Looking over Sam's shoulder Jory could see the signature of Pirate Davy

Dreadlocks. He also heard Mr Fizz mutter under his breath, 'Well that proves it.'

Jory didn't care if it proved it or not, he was convinced they would all be rich. He imagined himself walking along the harbour with a fine gold jacket and a hat with pearls around the brim and Mazy standing there and watching him and smiling.

'When are we going captain?' asked Sam.

'Soon very soon. I have to speak with Mr Lost and chart a course. Probably a zigzag one in case we are watched or followed. You'll get your orders soon enough. Right then Mr Lost if you would join me in my cabin.' With that, the captain rolled up the treasure map and set off for his cabin closely followed by Mr Lost.

Jory heard a rumble of thunder outside and realised he

had completely forgotten about the storm outside.

'Sounds like it's still blowing out there,' he said.

'I reckon that's a -blowing all night,' replied Sam. 'Best get your head down.'

Jory crawled back into the sail locker. Storm had found himself a comfortable sail and was asleep and purring loudly. Jory lay down next to the cat and drifted off to sleep thinking of piles of treasure.

Chapter Six

FeeBe goes missing.

Mazy could hear the rain bouncing off the roof of their cottage. 'Are we going to be all right?' she asked her Dad as the thunder crashed and boomed overhead.

'We'll be fine, Mazy. Nothing to be alarmed about. We've had plenty of storms before.'

'I worry about the animals outside,' said Mazy. 'Will they be all right too?'

'Don't you go worrying about them Mazy. Animals are used to the weather. I daresay they'll find some shelter somewhere, a hedge or a tree.'

'Is FeeBe in?' asked Mazy suddenly realising she hadn't seen her cat.

'FeeBe?' her mother said absently as she folded up a sheet she had been ironing. 'Now you mention it, I don't think I've seen her.'

'FeeBe, FeeBe,' called Mazy as she searched around the floor of the cottage.

'Maybe she's gone upstairs, in your bedroom. Probably afraid of the storm.'

Mazy ran upstairs to her bedroom. The cat was nowhere to be seen. Mazy looked under her bed and her bedclothes. She looked behind the small cupboard. Mazy's bedroom was tiny but FeeBe wasn't there. Mazy crossed over the stairs to her parents' bedroom.

'FeeBe, she called but there was no answering meow. Mazy looked around the bedroom but it was soon clear FeeBe wasn't in there either.

'Did you find her?' called her mother from downstairs.

'No,' said Mazy. 'I can't see her anywhere.'

The thunder rolled and boomed again and a huge flash of lightning made Mazy jump. Looking out of the window she watched the rain pouring down in great sheets of water. The rain was so heavy it was streaming down the pathway outside and falling down the steps towards the harbour. Mazy began to feel panic in her chest. What if FeeBe was caught somewhere outside in the storm. What if she was washed into the harbour? It was too horrible to think about.

Mazy went back downstairs. 'She's not upstairs, I've looked everywhere. I'm really worried about her.'

'She'll be fine,' said her Dad. 'Cat's got nine lives and in any case, she knows the ways around here, she'll have found somewhere to shelter.'

Mazy grabbed her coat from the coat hook. 'I'm going out to look for her.' Thunder growled around the cottage and rumbled away in the distance.

'You'll do no such thing,' ordered her mother. 'You are not going out in weather like this. Be patient, like your father says, FeeBe is quite capable of looking after herself.'

Mazy held the coat tightly to her chest and scowled. She knew it made sense to stay inside but she was so worried about FeeBe and she hated to be sitting still. She wanted to be doing something. She sat by the window and watched the rain falling from the dark sky. Lightning still flashed but not so brightly.

'Do cats really have nine lives,' she asked out loud still

wondering if FeeBe may have been washed into the harbour and drowned.

'Maybe they do and maybe they don't,' replied her father, poking the fire and getting it to blaze. A shower of red sparks burst from a log and shot up the chimney. 'But your FeeBe,' he continued, 'is a lucky cat. Don't you remember it was you who found and rescued her?'

'I want to go and rescue her again,' said Mazy peering out of the window.

'She'll be right, don't you worry. Now come and have some supper. Your mother's made us a hot stew with some potatoes.'

Mazy sat down with her mum and dad at the table but her stomach was tied in knots thinking about FeeBe. 'I'm not very hungry,' she said.

'Don't be daft Mazy,' said her mother. 'You have to eat something. Wouldn't be any good if FeeBe turned up in the morning only to find you starved to death would it now?'

Mazy took a mouthful of the stew. It did taste very nice. Her mother made the best stew. She began to feel better and decided FeeBe was probably in someone else's house and being kept fed and warm. She finished off her stew and sat down by the warmth of the fire.

'Do you know someone called Jehoshaphat?' she asked her father. Her father didn't reply. She sensed there was a pause; like an unspoken something.

Her father poked the fire again, 'Now where would you have heard of a name like that?'

Mazy decided not to say she had seen the name on her

uncle's ship, carved on the table. There was something not quite right about the way her father had answered her.

'Oh I heard some of the sailors talking and I overheard one of them talk about a sailor named Jehosaphat. I wondered if you knew him.'

'I did hear of one Jehoshaphat who lived in the village but it was a long time ago. Before you was born.' her father replied.

'What was he like?'

'Not he, she.'

Mazy's eyes went wide. 'She?' she said as though she didn't believe her father. Surely Jehoshaphat must have been a man. Captain Jehoshaphat the Terrible was the name carved in the table. He couldn't have been a woman. No women were allowed on the ship.

'What's wrong with that?' asked her father.

'No, nothing,' said Mazy hastily, her mind running as fast as it could. Could there have been another Jehoshaphat? If Jehoshaphat had been a pirate and The Black Booger had once been named The Scarlet Arrow then there must have been two Jehoshaphat's. But her father would surely have known that. She didn't like to ask again. She sat quietly thinking to herself but she was bursting with curiosity. One more question she thought.

'Did Uncle Henry know Jehoshaphat?' she asked not looking at her father so as not to appear too inquisitive.

The cottage went quiet. Her father poked at the fire, 'I daresay he might have done but it's not likely, as he was never in port in those days. Always off on some fool adventure.'

Mazy knew from the tone of her father's voice he wasn't telling the whole truth but he must have had his reasons. Mazy decided this was too interesting to leave alone but she would speak to Melwyn in the morning and together they would find out the secret about the mysterious Mr. or Mrs. Jehoshaphat.

Mazy lay wide awake in her bed listening to the rain bouncing off the roof of the cottage. The thunder had drifted away into the distance but Mazy still couldn't sleep. Her mind was buzzing with questions. Who was Jehoshaphat the Terrible and how did her uncle end up with his ship? And why did he change the name to The Black Booger? And why was the table cursed? Too many unanswered questions had to wait until the morning and Mazy rolled over and went to sleep dreaming of a wet black cat sailing a black ship.

The following morning the storm had passed and the sunlight streaming through the window woke up Mazy from a deep sleep.

'Breakfast!' shouted her mother.

Mazy clattered down the stairs and as she entered the kitchen she said, 'Is FeeBe back yet?'

'I haven't seen her,' replied her mother who was stirring a saucepan of porridge. 'Come and sit down and have something to eat before you go to school.'

Mazy sat down at the table and blew on her bowl of steaming porridge, 'I need to find FeeBe, I want to make sure she's all right.'

'You can look out for her on your way to school,' said her mum as she sat down at the table alongside Mazy. 'But I wouldn't worry she's bound to turn up.'

Mazy finished off her porridge and gathered up her school books. She did think of not going to school to search for FeeBe but she knew Mrs Scroggin would call on her parents if she missed school again.

'Say hi to Melwyn,' her mother called after her as Mazy set off.

The sun was shining and the ground was steaming. Mazy headed down the path towards the harbour. She looked everywhere for the missing FeeBe but the cat was nowhere to be seen. She saw Melwyn coming towards her so she shouted, 'Have you seen FeeBe anywhere?'

'No, why, is she missing?' said Melwyn as she caught up with her friend.

'She's been out all night in the storm and I can't find her anywhere.'

'Oh she'll be all right, cats always are.' replied Melwyn, swinging her school bag over one shoulder.

'That's what my parents kept telling me but I think something's happened to her,' replied Mazy heading towards the Crab and Crossed Claws.

Melwyn stopped walking and said after the departing Mazy, 'That's not the way to school. You'll be in trouble if you miss another day.'

'I'm just going to have a look,' said Mazy. 'You don't have to wait for me.'

Melwyn watched her friend walking away and sighed. Mazy was her best friend but she didn't want her in trouble. 'I'll come and help for a minute but we must get to school.'

She caught up with Mazy outside The Crab and Crossed Claws. Mr Borlaise was sat outside watching the seagulls. He looked up when the two girls appeared in front of him and said, 'Hello you two, shouldn't you be at school?'

'Yes we should,' said Mazy, 'but I've lost my cat FeeBe. You haven't seen her have you?'

'Black cat is she?' inquired Mr Borlaise looking up at Mazy from underneath his bushy eyebrows.

'Yes,' said Mazy. 'Have you seen her?'

'Well I've seen a cat that's black but it might not be

your cat of course.'

'Of course she's my cat. She's the only black cat around here,' said Mazy.

Melwyn tugged Mazy's sleeve. 'Come on we're going to be late.' She tried to pull Mazy away but Mazy was still talking to Mr Borlaise and wasn't going anywhere.

'Where did you see the black cat?' Mazy demanded.

Mr Borlaise shifted in his seat peered around Mazy and pointed in the direction of The Black Booger. 'Just before the storm, I seen a small, black cat, walk up the gangplank bold as anything.'

Mazy twisted around pulling against Melwyn's hand. She squinted in the sunlight and searched the deck of The Black Booger. There was no cat in sight.

'Come on Mazy,' urged Melwyn, 'we'll be late.'

'I'm not going without FeeBe,' replied Mazy firmly.

'But FeeBe's fine. She probably sheltered from the storm and she'll come home when she's ready,' persisted Melwyn tugging her bag back over her arm. Melwyn stared at Mazy and saw the determined frown on her face and realised school was the last thing on Mazy's mind. 'We're going to be in so much trouble,' she said.

Mazy didn't look round but continued to study the deck of The Black Booger. 'You can go, but I'm not leaving my cat on that ship.'

'What are you going to do?' asked Melwyn already suspecting Mazy fully intended going aboard to look for FeeBe.

'I am going to get my cat back. You can go to school

and tell Mrs Scroggin that I am very ill and my parents are not to be disturbed on account they are very worried about me.'

Melwyn looked at Mr Borlaise who had been listening to the conversation.

'Ho, don't look at me,' he said, 'not my cat.'

Mazy started to walk towards the harbour. 'Wait for me,' said Melwyn, and dropped her bag alongside Mr Borlaise. 'Look after that for me,' she said and followed on after Mazy.

'Oi, you two,' Mr Borlaise called out. 'I wouldn't be going straight up the gangplank, you'll be seen.'

Mazy and Melwyn stopped and turned around. 'Well how are we supposed to get on board?' asked Mazy.

Mr Borlaise shifted his cap back, scratched the top of

his head and said, 'If I was small like you two and I wanted to climb on board secretly then I would first get down into the smaller fishing boats in the harbour, walk across them to where they lie alongside and see if I could sneak in through one of the porthole windows in the side of the ship. That's what I would do. But I'm not telling you that's what you should do and I'll deny it if I'm ever asked.'

'Thank you,' grinned Mazy, 'we won't tell.'

The small fishing boats swayed and wobbled as Mazy and Melwyn clambered across them to reach the side of The Black Booger. Mazy stretched up on tiptoe and looked in through one of the round open windows on the side of the pirate ship. 'Can you see anything?' whispered Melwyn.

'It's too dark,' replied Mazy. 'Give me a leg up.'

Melwyn lifted Mazy and watched her disappear, head first, through the open window. 'Can you see FeeBe anywhere?' Melwyn whispered loudly.

Mazy's head appeared out of the window. 'She's not here, come on up and help me find her.'

'Ooh, I don't know. Can't you look? I don't want to get into any trouble.' Melwyn glanced around her as she spoke to Mazy. The port was quiet although there was the sound of low voices coming from inside The Black Booger.

'I need you to help me,' insisted Mazy. 'It'll be quicker if we both look. Grab my hand, I'll pull you up.'

Mazy stretched her arm down towards Melwyn. 'Do you think it's safe?' said Melwyn as she allowed Mazy to drag her up the side of the ship. 'No it's not safc,' giggled Mazy as they both fell into the small cabin.

'We'll probably get thrown to the sharks if they catch us.'

'There aren't any sharks here,' said Melwyn as she untangled herself from Mazy.

'Well, we've got nothing to worry about, have we?'

The two girls stood up and looked around them. Melwyn wrinkled her nose, 'It's a bit pongy. How could you live on a ship that smelt this bad?'

'Shhh,' cautioned Mazy, 'I can hear someone outside.'

They stood still and listened to the sound of footsteps coming closer and closer.

Melwyn stared at the door and grabbed her friend tightly by the arm as she saw the handle turning and the door opening.

A shadowy figure appeared in the doorway, suddenly jumped backwards and fell onto the floor. 'You idiot,' he exclaimed, 'you frightened the living ghosts out of me. What are you doing down here?'

Mazy bent forward, 'Jory?'

'Yes,' said Jory crossly, getting to his feet. 'It's Mazy right?'

'And Melwyn,' said Melwyn peering around Mazy where she had been trying to hide.

'What are you two doing?' said Jory, closing the door. 'Your uncle will kill you if he finds you on his ship. You know what he's like; you'll bring bad luck to all of us.'

'I'm not bad luck and I don't want to spend any more time than I have to on his smelly old ship. Once I have

FeeBe we'll be off and gone and no one will be any the wiser. Not unless you plan to snitch on us.'

'I won't snitch on you as long as you leave now and never mention this again. Look I'll help you back out of the porthole.'

'That seems fair, Mazy,' offered Melwyn, 'perhaps we should leave and Jory won't get into trouble either.'

Mazy placed her hands on her hips and stood right in front of Jory. 'I am not going, without FeeBe.'

Jory stared at her, frowning hard, 'Who is FeeBe?'

'FeeBe is my cat and Mr Borlaise saw her come on the ship last night, and I'm not leaving without her.'

'There's no cat on this ship,' said Jory beginning to think maybe Storm wasn't a stray cat after all but he had no intention of giving his cat up.

'Well, I'm still going to look for her.'

'You can't,' said Jory looking frightened for the first time.

'Why not?' demanded Mazy.

'Shh,' hushed Jory. 'If you're seen onboard the captain will be as mad as a bag of cross lobsters. He'll throw you overboard and I'll get thrown off too.'

Mazy squinted hard at Jory. She was really angry inside but she knew he was making sense and her uncle would be furious and her mum and dad would be furious and Mrs Scroggin would, well she would be something that wasn't nice.

'Um,' ventured Melwyn cautiously from behind Mazy's back, 'Maybe, Mazy, we could ask Jory to look for FeeBe, now he knows. Then we could go and we wouldn't be in trouble and Jory wouldn't be in trouble and he could find FeeBe and bring her back.'

'Now that's a good idea,' agreed Jory looking at Mazy for her to agree as well.

And Mazy would have reluctantly agreed had it not been for the sound of a cat's meow inside the cabin. No one said a word. Jory held his breath. Melwyn's eyes went wide. Mazy began to have horrible thoughts of what she would like to do to Jory.

'No cat on board?' she said icily.

'Well, what I meant was there was no cat on board belonging to you,' replied Jory lamely.

Mazy wasn't interested in Jory's excuse. She started calling out, 'FeeBe, FeeBe.'

A black cat peered out from between the folded sails

and went meow again.

'FeeBe, it is you,' cried Mazy and scooped up the cat.

'That's not your cat,' said Jory trying to take the cat from Mazy.

'Of course it's my cat. Whose cat do you think it is?' Mazy replied as she twisted away from Jory.

'He's mine,' said Jory, 'and his name is Storm,' still trying to take the cat away from Mazy.

'*His* name is Storm?' laughed Mazy. Melwyn giggled in the background.

'Why is that so funny?' said Jory angrily. 'It's a perfectly good name. I found him in the storm so that's his name.'

Jory continued to try and take the cat off Mazy who

was twisting backwards and forwards to avoid him.

'Oh poor Jory,' teased Mazy, 'you don't know much about cats do you.' She continued to laugh which made Jory more annoyed. He went to grab the cat which, by this time, had had enough of being fought over and wriggled free from Mazy's grasp and disappeared into the folded sails.

'Oh drat, look what you made me do,' said Mazy dropping onto her knees and calling, 'FeeBe, FeeBe.'

Melwyn was grinning at Jory.

'What's so funny?' he demanded.

'FeeBe is a girl cat and that's a girl cat. That's FeeBe,' replied Melwyn gleefully.

Kneeling on the cabin floor Mazy lifted the edge of one of the sails still calling to FeeBe.

There was the sound of running footsteps above them. Voices could be heard shouting urgently. 'What's going on?' asked Melwyn.

'I don't know,' replied Jory, 'It sounds like the crew are doing something. I'd better go and see if I'm needed.' He looked down at Mazy and said, 'Just find your stupid cat and leave as quickly as you can.'

'Oh don't worry,' replied Mazy still lifting the sails, 'I wouldn't want to stay another minute longer on this smelly ship than I have to.'

The smelly ship rocked.

 Mazy fell over and Jory and Melwyn staggered.

'We're moving!' exclaimed Melwyn and rushed to the open window. 'We are!' she screamed, 'We moving. Mazy, we're moving, the ship's leaving; we've got to get off now.'

'I haven't got FeeBe yet,' said Mazy as she scrambled to her feet.

'Never mind FeeBe,' shouted Melwyn. 'We've got to go now. Help me up.'

Mazy lifted her friend to the window and pushed her bottom to help shove her through the window.

'Stop, stop,' screamed Melwyn, 'stop pushing.'

'What is it?' asked Mazy from under Melwyn's skirt.

'I can't swim.'

Mazy let Melwyn drop back down and looked out of the window. With a sinking feeling in her stomach, she saw The Black Booger had left the harbour and was heading out to sea.

Melwyn slumped down on the cabin floor. 'What are we going to do?' she wailed 'We are in so much trouble and it's all your fault. You and that stupid cat.' Melwyn's chest heaved as she gave out a huge sob.

Mazy stared out of the window and watched the harbour slowly shrinking in size as The Black Booger picked up speed. Neither she nor Melwyn had learnt to swim and in any case, they were too far away from the land. She stepped away from the window and sat down next to her friend. She took Melwyn's hand in hers and said, 'I'm really sorry I got you into this Mellie, I didn't know the ship would leave.'

Melwyn sniffed loudly, 'It's all right I suppose, I agreed to come with you, but what are we going to do now?'

Mazy gave a big sigh, 'I'll just have to go and own up

to my uncle. We haven't gone far; maybe he can turn back and drop us off.'

Melwyn wiped the back of her hand across her eyes, 'Do you think so?'

Jory, who had been quiet said, 'That's never going to happen.'

Mazy and Melwyn looked up at him, 'Why's that?' asked Melwyn.

'For a start, you can't turn a ship this size around that easily and in any case, if you show yourselves to your uncle he will explode. He'll probably throw you overboard whether you can swim or not and he'll say the ships cursed, women on board bring bad luck and nobody will sail with him again and then he'll throw me overboard.'

'Well what do you suggest we do?' asked Mazy.

'I don't know right this minute. Let me think about it. But for the moment stay in the cabin out of sight.'

Jory left them in the cabin and went up to the deck wondering what he could do, or who he could ask as to how he was going to keep two girls onboard until they returned to Charlestown.

Mr Borlaise scratched the top of FeeBe's head as he watched The Black Booger make its way out of the harbour.

'Wonder where that fool captain's off to now,' he said to himself.

'What do you think Mrs Cat? Think he'll come back with Davy Dreadlocks treasure?'

Mr Borlaise knew all about the treasure map. He should do, he helped draw it.

'Think I should tell them girls parents they have gone on a jolly adventure, and I'll take you 'ome too.' Mr Borlaise heaved his body off the seat outside The Crab and Crossed Claws, gathered up FeeBe in his huge hand, Melwyn's school bag in the other, and headed up the path as The Black Booger became smaller and smaller in the distance.

Chapter Seven

Stowaways!

The Black Booger rolled and swayed as it headed out to sea. Mazy and Melwyn could hear the waves slapping against the side of the ship and seagulls screeching away in the distance.

The smell in the cabin didn't seem quite so bad and they had made themselves as comfortable as they could on the folded sails.

'Do you think your uncle would really throw us overboard?' asked Melwyn.

'I don't know,' replied Mazy, 'but he did get angry when I asked if I could go with him on one of his adventures. I don't know what he might do if he found us here.'

Melwyn stood up and looked out of the window. 'I can't see the land anymore we must be a long way from the shore already.'

Mazy joined Melwyn, 'Jory will think of something,' she said trying to comfort her friend. 'It will turn out all right, everything does in the end.'

'I'm not so sure this time. My mum and dad will be so angry and we'll be thrown out of school for certain. Then what shall we do?'

'I don't care if I didn't go back to Mrs Scroggin's class. She's so mean and horrible. I'll get a job at the harbour, maybe fixing the nets or going fishing. I could get some money to give to my mum so she didn't have such a hard time.'

Melwyn sat back down on the sails, 'That's not what I

want; I want to study and be a Doctor and help make people better.'

'But you'll be at school forever and ever,' said Mazy.

'It's not forever but it is a long time. Mrs Scroggin says I could do it if I study hard and pass top in my exams. She says sometimes the higher school will take a top student and help with the cost.'

'Wow,' said Mazy. 'You'll do it I know you will and you'd be a brilliant Doctor.'

'Thank you for saying that,' Melwyn said sadly looking around the cabin, 'but I don't think any of that will happen now. Not when everyone finds out we ran away to sea.'

'I know,' exclaimed Mazy, 'we'll say we were kidnapped. Pirates do that all the time. Kidnapping people and selling them as slaves or making them work painting the ship or something. Then it won't be our fault at all.'

Melwyn laughed. Although she felt unhappy Mazy had a habit of always coming up with something crazy that made her laugh.

'Crazy Mazy, you are so silly.'

'Why? I think it's a great plan.' said Mazy full of enthusiasm.

'Well, there is the small thing of Mr Borlaise telling us how to get on board without being seen. And then him watching us. And then Jory finding us. I don't think anyone will believe we were kidnapped.'

'Drat,' said Mazy dropping down to sit next to Melwyn. 'See, that's why you can be a Doctor, your just so smart.'

They both heard the sound of footsteps approaching.

'Should we hide?' whispered Melwyn.

Mazy held her finger up to her lips, staring at the door. They watched as the handle slowly turned and the door opened. Jory poked his head through.

'Oh, it's only you,' said Mazy breathing out.

'I've got someone with me though,' replied Jory pushing the door open. He entered the cabin followed by a short fat man with curly ginger hair.

'Oh Ho,' the man said, raising his eyebrows as he peered down at Mazy and Melwyn. 'What do us have here but a couple of stowaways no doubt.'

'We're not stowaways,' corrected Mazy. 'We didn't want to be here.'

The man scratched the side of his face, 'Then why are you here, if not to sail on a pirate adventure?'

'We came after a cat,' explained Melwyn.

'A cat you say. The only cat onboard The Black Booger is Jory's cat.'

'She's not Jory's cat!' said Mazy. 'She's my cat!'

The man glanced across at Jory who was stood by the door looking dejected. 'Jory, you got a cat,'

'Please Gruntle, don't make it worse. I told you it was a mistake. I just want to know how we can get Mazy and Melwyn back without the captain finding out.'

'Gruntle?' inquired Mazy.

'An' what's wrong with that?' said Gruntle.

'Ah, nothing, nothing,' stammered Mazy, 'it's just an

unusual name; I've not heard it before and I thought I knew everyone on my uncle's ship.'

'Oh, that's right,' said Gruntle shrugging his shoulders and thrusting his hands into his pockets. 'I know you Mazy and I know the captain's your uncle. I also know if he finds you on board his ship he'll cut you up into tiny pieces and throw you to the seagulls or sharks as food.'

The conversation was interrupted by a loud wail from Melwyn who burst into tears.

'I don't want to be cut up into tiny pieces,' she sobbed.

'Now look what you've done,' said Mazy placing her arms around her friend to comfort her. 'You should be ashamed, picking on two little girls like that.'

'Sorry, sorry, I didn't mean to be upsetting you,'

apologised Gruntle quickly. 'Here have my hanky and dry your eyes.' He pulled out a crumpled, dirty, blue and white cloth from his pocket and offered it to Mazy.

Mazy looked at the hanky and screwed up her face. 'Um, that's very kind but Melwyn's ok, thank you.'

Jory interrupted their conversation, 'What are we going to do with them, Gruntle?'

Gruntle straightened up, wiggled his nose backwards and forwards as he gave it some thought. 'First of, have you had any food yet?'

'We haven't had anything,' said Mazy, wondering why food was suddenly important but happy to eat anything that was on offer.

'Right oh, wait there, I'll go get us something to eat,' said Gruntle. He pushed past Jory and was gone.

Mazy looked at Jory and said, 'Why does he think we need feeding? Not that I mind,' she continued hastily, never one to turn down food when it was on offer.

'He's Gruntle, the ship's cook. He feeds everybody.'

The Black Booger suddenly leant over to one side. Jory grabbed the side of the door to steady himself. Mazy and Melwyn rolled across the floor. 'Ow,' said Mazy, as she banged her arm on a pile of sails.

Jory looked up at the ceiling and tilted his head to one side, 'That's odd; I think we've just changed course.'

The Black Booger swayed and swerved through the water. Jory staggered from side to side trying to keep his balance. Mazy stood up and looked out of the window. Seaspray burst through the air as the ship rose and fell in the water. The wind blew through the window and Mazy could smell the salt of the sea.

'Look,' she said. 'There's land not far away.'

Jory staggered over to join her and looked out of the window. 'We must be going alongside the coast and not out to sea.' explained Jory. 'We're heading for Lands End,'

The ship gave a hard lurch and a wave rolled alongside the side of the ship and sprayed saltwater over Jory and Mazy. They moved back and Mazy sat down next to Melwyn again. 'Ooh,' said Mazy, 'you look a funny colour, a bit green.'

'I feel green,' muttered Melwyn. 'I don't think I like being at sea.'

The door opened and Gruntle entered followed by a tall skinny man who was wearing a blue woolly hat.

Gruntle carried two small bowls of hot soup, one he handed to Mazy and the other to Melwyn. 'There you go,' he said, in a friendly way. 'Skirtle's got the spoons.'

The tall skinny man, who Gruntle had introduced as Skirtle, handed a spoon to Mazy and one to Melwyn.

'We've had a meeting,' commenced Gruntle, 'Me, and the rest of the crew excepting of course the captain and Mr Lost the navigator, and we have a plan.'

'Isa good plan,' said Skirtle joining in. 'Yous going to be newly recruited pirate trainees just to see how you'd fit in and whether you'd be any good to go with us full time.'

'But the captain doesn't like girls,' said Mazy.

'And I don't want to be cut up into tiny pieces,' added

Melwyn who was looking a whole lot better now she had eaten some of the soup.

'We'll make sure you keep out of the way and we'll disguise you to look like sailors. Dress you up right in some old sailor type clothes,' replied Gruntle.

'An you can have one of my hats to hide your hair' said Skirtle, grinning at them as if this was the greatest idea ever.

'Then you'll be able to move about the ship,' continued Gruntle. 'We'll get you to do stuff 'cause everyone has to work while they're on board. Nothing too hard, help with the cooking and cleaning the decks and stuff. What do you say to that?'

'How long,' began Melwyn slowly, 'will we be away from home?'

Gruntle glanced at Skirtle who looked down at his boots and looked at Jory. No-one said anything.

Jory said, 'Can you two keep a secret?'

'Course we can,' replied Mazy, nudging her friend in the side. 'Can't we Melwyn?'

'I don't know we should be telling them, Jory,' interrupted Skirtle. 'I mean it's a kind of pirates secret. They ain't pirates, they're stowaways.'

'They're not stowaways; they're going to be part of the crew so they should know.' said Jory. He turned to face Mazy and Melwyn and took a deep breath, 'We're going to search for Davy Dreadlocks treasure.'

Melwyn snorted. Then she giggled. Then she burst out laughing.

Skirtle scratched his head and even Gruntle stopped

smiling for a moment.

Jory frowned at her. 'What's so funny?'

'Davy Dreadlocks treasure,' giggled Melwyn. 'Please don't tell me the captain has a map of an island where the treasure is buried?'

Skirtle stared at her, 'What do you know about Davy Dreadlocks treasure map?'

'Well,' she started, 'I know that it's not real.'

'Oh no,' groaned Gruntle.

'It must be real,' said Skirtle, 'The captain had to fight a dozen men to get hold of it. How can it not be real?'

'Because,' continued Melwyn, 'I helped to draw it with Mr Borlaise.'

Chapter Eight

Davy Dreadlocks Treasure Island.

The Black Booger shifted and rolled through the waves. The crew climbed up the rigging and adjusted the sails so they caught the most wind. The front of the ship rose and fell down into the sea sending a fine spray of seawater back across the deck. Seagulls floated on the wind behind the ship looking out for any scraps of food that might be thrown overboard.

Mazy climbed up to the top of the stairs and stepped out onto the deck. She paused and looked all around her to see if her uncle was in view. She saw him standing at the rear of the ship holding onto the large steering wheel. He was gripping it with both of his hands and staring far into the distance. Mazy wondered how he could know which direction to steer the ship. Jory was already out on deck and he waved at her. Mazy ducked down behind some barrels and quickly made her way to Jory's side using him to hide her from her uncle's sight. Jory looked her up and down as he tried not to laugh at her appearance.

She was dressed in a pair of dirty blue trousers that were too large for her but held up with string tied around her waist. Gruntle had lent her a red and white stripy shirt which she had tucked inside the trousers, but the wind was trying to turn it into a giant sail. On her head was a small black, woollen hat. Gruntle had also rubbed some soot, from his stove, onto her face.

'You look pretty convincing,' said Jory.

They were on deck holding onto the side to keep their balance against the rocking of the ship.

Mazy kept looking all around her. 'It's ok,' said Jory, 'your uncle's at the back. How's Melwyn getting on?'

'She's still trying things on. She's a bit more fussy than me. She's still worried we're going to be found out.'

'If you two keep out of the way, you should be fine.'

Seawater splashed over the front of the ship as it rose and fell through the waves. She peered through the spray, 'Is that an island in the distance?'

Jory looked forward and squinted his eyes, 'I think you're right. I wonder if that's where the captain's treasure map is taking us.'

The Black Booger shuddered and heaved violently sideways. Mazy heard someone shout. She looked around and saw her uncle shading his eyes and staring out into the distance.

'Is my uncle actually blind?' she asked beginning to suspect that he could see as well as anyone.

Jory didn't reply. He was also staring out ahead at the approaching island.

She turned her back on her uncle and leant out over the side of the ship to see what the fuss was about. She could see a small dark shape far ahead of them. Looking back at Jory she asked, 'Is that *the* island?'

Jory wiped the sea spray from his face, 'I think so. I'll bet that's where we are heading, to look for Davy Dreadlocks treasure.'

'Careful boy,' boomed a voice coming from behind them. Blind Lightning Henry had left his position on the wheel and come forward. He hung onto one of the ropes and leant over Jory to stare at the island in the distance. Mazy shrunk down alongside Jory trying to make herself as small and invisible as possible. She didn't need to worry as her uncle was more interested in the island coming into view. She looked up at him and could see he was staring intently. She realised he wasn't blind at all; it was all an act just like his stories. She clenched her fists in anger remembering all the times she had guided him around the harbour to stop him falling in and listened to his stories about fighting the sea dragon and sharks. She wanted to shout at him, 'You fraud!' but she couldn't. She was sure he would throw her overboard if he found her on his ship.

'LAND HO!' shouted a loud voice from the top of one of the masts.

Captain Blind Lightning Henry craned his neck upwards and shouted back, 'It's been there for the last ten minutes. Tell me something I don't know.'

There was a pause.

'It's long and thin and jaggedey,' replied the voice.

'Of course it is,' said the captain. 'That's exactly how the map describes the island. We're going to be rich, boys. Davy Dreadlocks treasure's there for the taking.'

Mazy wriggled away from Jory and the captain trying to keep herself as small as possible. She expected to hear her uncle shout after her but the only sound was the wind banging the sails and the waves beating up along the side of the ship. Once she was out of sight of her uncle Mazy breathed a deep sigh. On the other side of the ship, she saw a small boy in a long, bright red jumper and boots that looked too big for him. His head was covered by a dirty brown floppy hat. She walked towards the boy and wondered why she hadn't seen him before. She knew all the crew that sailed with her uncle. Could this person be trusted not to give her and Melwyn away? What if he sounded the alarm? Her heart began to beat faster as she tried to keep out of sight behind some barrels. Her foot caught on a loop of rope lying on the deck and she stumbled. She grabbed the edge of the barrel and steadied herself but she had made too much noise to go unnoticed.

The boy turned around and looked straight at Mazy, 'What do you think of my disguise?'

Mazy stared. It wasn't a boy at all. Her heart gave a skip as she realised it was Melwyn.

'Ooh you gave me such a start,' she exclaimed walking up to her friend who was grinning at her from under the brim of the hat.

'What do you think?' asked Melwyn.

'It's brilliant,' said Mazy. 'I thought you were a boy from the back. And we're going to need good disguises because my uncle isn't blind at all.'

'I didn't think he was,' said Melwyn. 'Gruntle hinted at it as he found me these clothes. I asked him why did we need to dress up if the Captain couldn't see us and that's when he said, 'Don't believe everything you hear about pirates.''

'Well, he was right. My uncle's been staring at the island ahead of us convinced that's where Davy Dreadlocks treasure is buried. Did you really draw the map with Mr Borlaise?'

'It was Mr Borlaise mainly. I just added some whales and fishes and stuff to make it look more like it should.'

Mazy stared at the island. She wondered if she should tell her uncle that the map was a fake; and his hunt for the treasure was a waste of time. She thought about all the times he had pretended he was blind and made her guide him around the port to The Crab and Crossed Claws. He deserved to be fooled just like he had done to her. She rested her arms on the edge of the rail overlooking the front of the ship and watched the waves break and roll over the sharp rocks which surrounded the island.

'Melwyn, do you think we are getting too close to the rocks out there?'

Melwyn leant forward alongside her, 'They do look close and we don't seem to be changing course.'

Mazy wondered if whoever was steering the ship had seen the rocks. She saw Jory making his way towards them. 'There are rocks ahead,' she warned him.

'I know,' he replied, 'I've got to help see a way through. Shout out what I tell you.'

He scrambled over the front of the ship and crawled out on the mast that jutted out in front of the ship. Mazy watched Jory as he sat astride the mast, the waves breaking over him as the ship dipped and rose again through the water.

'Go left!' shouted Jory.

Mazy turned around and shouted at the top of her voice, 'GO LEFT!'

She felt the ship shudder under her feet and slowly turn to the left.

'Straight on.'

'STRAIGHT ON!'

The ship moved again. Mazy saw a huge jagged rock pass by them on the right-hand side.

Jory shouted again, 'Go right, go right.'

Mazy turned around towards the back of the ship and yelled out the instruction.

'GO RIGHT! GO RIGHT!' Jory's voice sounded full of alarm.

Mazy heard a loud scraping noise from the front of the ship as it began to make its turn.

'We've hit a rock,' shouted Melwyn. 'We're going to be shipwrecked.'

Mazy ran to the left-hand side of the ship and saw another huge jagged rock sliding past them rubbing against the hull of the ship. Pieces of wood were flying off the side as the ship rolled away from the dangerous rocks.

She saw the sails were coming down and felt the ship slowing as it swung to the right. Ahead was a calm area of sea which didn't appear to have any rocks but she knew they could easily be hidden under the water. The ship was slowing down and heading for the calmer water. Jory scrambled back onto the deck and looked over the side of the ship where it had struck the rock. 'That was close. I thought we'd had it. Looks like we just scraped it a bit; no sign of us sinking.'

Sam and Dave joined them to peer over the side. 'Don't look too bad,' said Dave.

'Don't look too bad,' said Sam.

'Gotta get the anchor out, Jory,' said Dave.

'Anchor out,' said Sam.

The Black Booger swung round in the wind its sails flapping, as it slowed down. Dave, Sam and Jory released the anchor which flew down into the sea with a great splash. The deck shook as the anchor caught on the bottom of the sea bed and pulled the ship up to a standstill.

Mazy looked towards the island, which was a short distance away from where they had stopped. She could see one or two small, sandy beaches backed by tall cliffs. The cliffs were covered in sea birds. Seagulls flew round in tight circles and smaller birds hopped and jumped along the edges. The tops of the cliffs were covered in grass and bushes with the odd tree all twisted by the wind.

Other members of the crew came forward to look over Davy Dreadlock's Treasure Island.

Mr Fizz held up his hand to shade his eyes from the sun. 'Looks like we could land a boat on one of those beaches.'

'Island looks awful big to find anything,' said Dave.

'Awful big,' said Sam.

'Yeah well, the captain's got a map,' joined in Gruntle.

Melwyn and Mazy glanced at each other. Mazy wondered if Gruntle had forgotten that Melwyn and Mr Borlaise had made the map and there was no treasure. She began to feel a bit sorry for the others as they thought they were going to become rich. Perhaps she should tell her uncle in some way and at least they might return home sooner than having to wait for them to search the whole of the island until they decided there was no treasure.

'Captain on the deck,' said Dave loudly.

'Captain on the deck,' repeated Sam.

Mazy turned around and saw her uncle striding towards them. She dropped down to sit on the deck and pulled her knees up to her chin to make herself as small and invisible as possible. Her uncle's boots were right in front of her.

'Treasure Island, lads,' boomed the captain. 'Just need Mr Lost to navigate us to the treasure and we'll all be rich. Well done Jory,' he continued, 'for that piece of navigating around the rocks, and who was helping you shout out. I didn't recognise the voice.'

Gruntle stood in front of Mazy so the Captain couldn't

see her, 'Ah, begging your pardon Captain, but we took a couple of youngsters on. See if they'd make a good crew like. Need some youngsters to train up.'

'Well where are they?' demanded the captain. 'Like to put a face to my crew so I know who's who.'

Gruntle moved sideways to reveal Mazy sat on the deck still with her head down. Melwyn sidled out from behind Mr Fizz, her hat pulled down over her face.

The crew waited in silence to see if Blind Lightning Henry would recognise the two girls and if he did would he admit to them he wasn't blind. Mazy could feel her heart thumping in her chest. Her mouth went dry when she heard her uncle say, 'You there, sat on the deck, stand up and let's have a look at you.'

Mazy stood up. She held her hands together in front of

her and kept her head down as low as she could.

The whole world seemed to have come to a standstill.

No one spoke.

Her uncle said quietly and slowly, 'Mazy Ansell.'

Chapter Nine

Sinking of The Black Booger.

Mazy looked up into her Uncle's eyes. He was staring hard at her. 'Who's your friend?' he asked.

Melwyn stepped forward before Mazy could say anything. 'Melwyn Nancekivell, sir.'

'Mazy and Melwyn,' he said. Then in a very loud voice, he repeated himself, 'Mazy and Melwyn.'

He looked around at the crew who, in turn, were all looking down at their feet and shuffling them two and fro. 'I take it,' continued Blind Lightning Henry in a loud voice, 'that you all knew about this?'

No one said a word.

Mazy saw her uncle's face had gone bright red. His

eyes were bulging and his hands were grasping his belt so tightly she thought he might snap it. Then he exploded.

'Haven't you learnt anything,' he shouted, stomping backwards and forwards in front of the crew. 'Never again, never again, we all agreed. Women is bad luck. Should never be on the ship. You know what will happen.' Blind Lightning Henry swept his captain's hat off his head and threw it onto the deck in exasperation. Left a bit, the parrot shrieked and flew off into the rigging.

'See,' continued the captain still shouting at the top of his voice, 'See, the parrot knows. Girls on a ship is very, very bad luck.' Mazy could see her uncle was getting very angry. Pointing at her he shouted, 'Over the side, they'll have to go, can't risk it.'

'What!' said Jory stepping forward, 'You can't do that.'

Blind Lightning Henry swung around towards Jory and hissed, 'Don't tell me what I can or can't do on my ship, boy. I suppose it was you who brought them on board so you can go over the side too.'

Mazy couldn't believe what she was hearing. She thought her uncle would be angry if he found them on his ship but she had also thought the suggestion he would throw them overboard was just a threat. It wouldn't actually happen. He couldn't possibly drown them for being on The Black Booger, could he?

'Begging your pardon, captain,' interrupted Gruntle. 'They haven't been any trouble and have worked hard and it was young Mazy who shouted out the directions so as we didn't hit the rocks.'

Mazy gave Gruntle a little smile to thank him for sticking up for them.

'You know what happened last time,' the captain snapped back. 'I said never again, didn't I and I mean it. They will bring us nothing but bad luck. Or don't you thieving lot want to get rich with Davy Dreadlocks treasure. 'Cause if they stay, there will be no treasure and like as not we'll all die a 'orrible death on the island.'

Mazy was about to try and find out from her uncle what it was that had happened before, that made him so afraid of having women on his ship but she was interrupted by Melwyn.

She took off her hat and said in a firm voice, 'If the only thing you're worried about is Davy Dreadlocks treasure I can put your mind at ease.'

Mazy stared at Melwyn in horror. If Melwyn told her uncle the map was a fake, there's no knowing how he would react.

The captain glared at her, 'And what do you know about Davy Dreadlocks treasure?'

'I know the map's not real. I know there is no Davy Dreadlocks and I know that there are two whales and two fishes and one sea serpent drawn on it.'

Blind Lightning Henry pushed his face right in front of Melwyn's, 'And how do you know that?'

Mazy hung her head. Some of the crew started to walk away in anticipation of Melwyn revealing she had helped Mr Borlaise draw the map. There would be no knowing what the captain might do when he discovered the truth.

Suddenly the whole world around Mazy exploded. She heard a gigantic cracking noise. She looked up and saw the mast had been smashed through the middle and was twisting and turning and falling towards her in a tangle of ropes and sails. Pieces of wood, some small and some large were bouncing off the deck. She became aware of Jory alongside her. He grabbed her around her waist and dragging her sideways pulled her down onto the deck near the barrels as the mast crashed down where she had just been standing.

'Melwyn,' she screamed trying to sit up and look for her friend.

'She's ok,' said Jory who had blood running down the side of his face where a splinter of wood had hit him. 'She's over there.'

'What just happened?' asked Mazy, watching Melwyn

crawling towards them in-between the tangle of ropes and broken timber.

'I don't know. I think we must be under attack from somewhere.'

Mazy could hear members of the crew shouting and calling to each other. Someone shouted, 'Look out there's something coming.'

A large rock, covered in grass, flew over the top of them and crashed into the sea, throwing up a huge fountain of water.

'Here comes another one,' shouted Jory. This one struck another one of the masts, snapping it in two like it was a twig. Mazy watched in horror as the top half of the mast spun around, but it was held up by the ropes wrapped around it. She could hear her uncle shouting,

'Pull the anchor up and let's get out of here.'

She and Jory scrambled to their feet. Mazy looked towards the island and saw a huge figure of a man standing on the edge of the cliff. He was at least as tall as the tallest mast on the ship. He had bright red hair and a big bushy beard and he was tearing up another large rock from the ground.

Sam and Dave came towards them, dragging the tangled ropes to one side, clearing the way to the anchor chain.

'Who is that?' asked Mazy pointing to the island.

'That'll be Ralph the Wrath,' replied Dave.

'Ralph the Wrath,' said Sam. He swivelled his head up and shouted, 'Here comes another one.'

They all ducked down as another huge rock sailed over

the top of them and crashed into the sea. Dave pushed the broken mast out of the way and said to Jory, 'Come on, give a hand here or we'll all be at the bottom of the ocean or worse Ralph will wade out and have us for his dinner.'

'Dinner,' said Sam.

Mazy and Melwyn joined in dragging the ropes out of the way. 'Who is Ralph the Wrath?' asked Melwyn.

'They say he's a Cornish giant that likes to sink ships to steal their gold and eat their crew. Never believed in it myself but there he is, big as anything.'

'Big as the island,' said Sam.

Dave, Sam and Jory released the rope holding the anchor.

Dave shouted towards the back of the ship, 'Anchor's

gone, let's go.'

Mazy glanced towards the island and could see another rock flying towards them. She shouted out a warning and they all looked to see where this rock was going to land.

It was coming straight for the ship.

Mazy felt herself being pushed violently sideways as the rock crashed through the centre of the deck. At the same time, she felt Melwyn fall with her. She tried to push away rope and bits of wood that were lying around her and untangle herself from Melwyn. But it wasn't Melwyn or rope that was holding her down it was her uncle's arms. He was lying on top of them with his arms wrapped around both of them. Mazy realised her uncle had saved their lives.

'Dave,' commanded her uncle as he stood up. 'Get the two girls and Jory into the lifeboat. Maybe they will be too small to be seen and they can escape.'

'Aye aye, captain,' replied Dave and, followed by Sam, he ran back along the ship to release a small rowing boat that was carried for an emergency.

Another large rock flew across over their heads and smashed into the deck. The ship leant over sharply and everything on the deck began sliding towards the water.

'Jory,' continued the captain, 'Take the lifeboat and Mazy and Melwyn and try to make towards the mainland. Hopefully you three at least can row away to safety.'

'What about you and the rest of the crew?' asked Mazy desperately.

'We'll have to take our chances. The rowboats not big enough for all of us. Now go.'

Blind Lightning Henry turned away and staggered back along the ship's deck, holding on to whatever was available as the ship was leaning further and further over to one side.

The Black Booger was sinking and there was nothing anyone could do to save her.

Jory pulled the small rowing boat alongside the edge of the deck which was now underwater.

'Come on,' he said. Mazy and Melwyn clambered into the boat. Jory jumped in after them and pushed the boat away from the side of the ship.

Mazy watched the crew falling and sliding into the sea, 'Can't we save anyone else? We can't just let them all drown.'

'We need to get away from the ship or it will drag us down with her when she sinks. Then we'll look for anyone we can help.' Jory pushed the rowing boat further away from the side of The Black Booger with an oar and began to row away from the ship. Mazy looked from end to end along the ship but could no longer see any of the crew.

Mazy felt sick to her stomach. Her hands hurt where she gripped the side of the little rowing boat so tightly. It's all my fault, she thought. I should never have gone on board. Her uncle was right. She and Melwyn had brought the most awful bad luck and as a result, her uncle and all the crew could drown. She searched and searched the water for any of the crew they could rescue but she couldn't see anyone.

She watched The Black Booger slowly sinking and couldn't believe what had happened. Her uncle was gone and all the crew and the ship. Tears sprang from her eyes and streamed down her face. As she watched The Black Booger slowly sinking another huge boulder smashed into it. The ship disintegrated in a shower of wood and ropes and barrels and torn sails and finally disappeared under the water. Mazy searched the surface of the water and could see several of the crew hanging onto floating pieces of wood. She was about to direct Jory towards them when Melwyn screamed, 'The giant's coming out into the sea.'

Mazy looked back towards the island and saw the giant wading out from the shore towards them. He was so tall the sea only reached up to his waist. He had a big club in one hand which he was waving from side to side.

Jory pulled on the oars and spun the little rowing boat around. He began pulling hard and the boat moved quickly away from where The Black Booger had sunk.

Mazy turned on him, 'What are you doing?'

'I'm getting us away. We can't save everybody and your uncle told me to take you and Melwyn to safety.' He looked over his shoulder and continued to row away from the wreckage. Mazy stared in disbelief as they moved further and further away. She saw the giant picking the crew out of the water and placing them into a sack.

'What's he doing?' asked Melwyn.

'I don't think he's rescuing them,' replied Jory.

'Remember what Dave said, he likes to eat people.'

Mazy frowned in concentration. 'We can still save them.'

'How are we going to do that?' asked Melwyn. 'He's huge and he'll eat us too.'

Ignoring her friend she turned to Jory. 'Can you get us to the island?'

'I'll try,' panted Jory who was rowing as hard as he could. Mazy and Melwyn watched anxiously as the giant splashed around in the sea still picking objects out of the water and placing them into his sack. Mazy hoped that everyone had been saved but at that moment she had no idea how she was going to rescue them. Mazy looked at the beach ahead of them and tried to see if there was a safe place to land. She could see several beaches but one had rocks surrounding it.

'Go there,' she commanded.

Jory looked at where Mazy was pointing. 'Why that one?'

'The rocks will give us somewhere to hide the boat and ourselves.'

Jory steered the rowing boat expertly around the rocks and the waves carried them up onto the beach. Mazy and Melwyn jumped out and held onto the front of the boat while Jory secured the oars. He jumped out next to them and helped them drag the boat further up the beach so it wouldn't float away.

'What now?' asked Melwyn.

Mazy didn't know. It seemed like a good idea to try and rescue her uncle and the rest of the crew but she had no idea how that was going to be possible. The beach they had landed on was surrounded by high cliffs. She looked up and saw seagulls flying around in circles above her head but no way to climb up. And if there was a way up they still had to find where the giant had taken the crew, rescue them, and escape, all without being eaten. Of all the ideas she had had this one had to be the craziest. Jory tied the boat to a rock to stop it from floating away. He looked along the beach and said, 'I can hear running water.'

Mazy walked out from behind the rocks to see where the sound was coming from. The three of them walked along the beach dodging the rock pools and clambering over the larger rocks. The beach turned out to be bigger than had first appeared. At the end of the beach, they came to a high jagged rock which extended out into the sea. They could still hear what sounded like a waterfall so they started to climb up over the rough surface. Jory was quicker than the two girls and arrived at the top of the rock first. Mazy looked up at him and saw that he had stopped and was staring into the distance. 'What can you see?' she called out to him.

'You'll have to see it for yourself. You won't believe it,' and he disappeared from view.

Mazy climbed up to the top and saw the beach continued on the other side. It was what was on the beach that made her stop in amazement.

'What is it?' asked Melwyn who was still climbing up behind her.

'It's a ship,' replied Mazy still not believing her eyes.

Chapter Ten

The Scarlet Arrow.

Jory was already down on the sand and making his way towards the ship.

Puffing and panting with the climb Melwyn finally arrived next to Mazy. 'That's amazing,' she exclaimed. 'It's like The Black Booger but smaller. Why do you think it's here?'

'No idea but if it's any good it may be our way to escape.' replied Mazy from over her shoulder as she made her way down to the beach.

The two girls ran along the beach towards the ship and Jory, who was waving his arms and pointing up at the front of the ship.

'He looks very excited,' gasped Melwyn, as she tried to keep up with her friend. 'I wonder what he's found.'

When Mazy and Melwyn caught up with Jory, Mazy said, 'Is it seaworthy? Will it float? Do you think we could push it into the sea? If we rescue everybody can we use it to escape?'

Jory laughed. 'So many questions but before all that, look,' and he pointed up to the front of the ship.

Mazy froze. Her mouth went dry. For a moment she couldn't speak. There, in large red letters carved along the front of the ship was its name.

The Scarlet Arrow.

She looked at Jory who was grinning at her. 'That's not possible, I thought The Black Booger was The Scarlet Arrow.'

'Come on,' said Jory, 'Let's have a look onboard. There's a ladder on the other side that doesn't look too rotten.'

Once on board the ship, Jory began examining the masts and ropes. 'If there is a decent set of sails I reckon she would sail. We would have to get her off the beach somehow and into the water.'

'Do you think this was Captain Jehoshaphat's ship?' asked Mazy.

'I don't know,' replied Jory. 'I thought The Black Booger was the ship and had its name changed. I'll go and have a look around and see if I can find anything else.'

Melwyn grabbed hold of Mazy's arm. 'What's this all about, Captain Jehoshaphat and The Scarlet Arrow?'

'There was a table in my uncle's cabin on The Black Booger which had carved on it, 'This table belongs to Captain Jehoshaphat the Terrible.' And according to Jory, Captain Jehoshaphat was a good friend of my uncle and The Black Booger was originally The Scarlet Arrow.' explained Mazy as she followed Jory down inside the ship.

'So how is this ship here and what happened to your uncle's friend?' Melwyn asked.

'I don't know. No one seems to know. I asked my dad and he got funny about answering my questions. He even said that Jehoshaphat was a woman. There's something strange about all of this.'

The inside of the ship was a tangle of small barrels and twisted rope which was covered in rotting seaweed. There were old bits of torn rag and cooking pots scattered along the floor. Small crabs waved their pincers at them. Pushing a broken chair to one side Mazy continued to follow Jory who had disappeared into a cabin at the rear of the ship.

''It stinks,' said Melwyn wrinkling up her nose. 'I wonder how long it's been here.'

'I don't know but it doesn't look too bad. I wonder if it would float.'

'Come in here,' Jory shouted.

The cabin was like her uncle's cabin but smaller. The first thing that struck Mazy was how empty it was except for a low bench along one side and a small table in the centre. There were piles of papers on the floor and dust everywhere. Crabs scuttled to one side as she walked over to the bench and sat down. Jory was looking at some of the papers he had picked up from the floor.

'Anything interesting?' asked Melwyn.

'They're just bills and old maps but look at this one.'

He handed it to Mazy, and Melwyn leant over her shoulder to have a look.

'Look at the signature on the bottom,' said Jory.

Mazy screwed up her eyes and peered hard at the faded writing. 'It says Jehoshaphat.'

'What does it mean?' asked Melwyn.

Jory pushed past them and headed for the doorway, 'Don't know, but I think we should see if we can rescue the crew. We've wasted enough time already.'

Melwyn followed him leaving Mazy alone inside the

cabin.

Mazy was lost in thought. There was something she should do but she couldn't think what it was. Something that Jory had said or done. What was it?

Then she remembered. Her uncle had a chest hidden in his cabin. She jumped up and looked carefully all around the small cabin. Where would you hide something where there was nowhere to hide? She was staring right at it; the bench she had been sat on. The top was loose. She lifted the top and saw a small wooden chest inside and next to the chest was a rolled-up map. Her heart thumping she opened the chest and lifted out a small, dirty brown bag.

'Come on Mazy.' Jory was shouting at her from outside.

She placed the bag in her pocket and glanced around the cabin in case she may have missed anything else. There was nothing else that caught her eye. She heard Jory calling to her from outside again so she left the cabin and climbed down the side of the ship to join Melwyn and Jory on the beach.

Melwyn looked at the rolled-up map in her hand and said, 'What have you got there?'

'It's a map, I think. I found it in the cabin.'

'Let's have a look,' said Jory. He took it from her and unrolled it. Mazy and Melwyn stood behind him as he held it up and they examined the map together. There were all sorts of marks and words scrawled all over it.

'What do you make of it?' asked Melwyn.

Jory rubbed under his nose and frowned. 'I think it's a

map of this island. This area here looks like the two coves we're in and this point is the top of the cliffs where we saw the giant Ralph the Wrath. There's some writing here but it's very faint.' He held it up to the light and peered at the map. Mazy stood on tiptoes to look over his shoulder.

'That word there says giant,' she said. 'You're right; this is a map of the island and look there, at the edge, does that say gold?'

Jory turned the map this way and that trying to make out the squiggly writing. 'You might be right, but it's difficult to make out.'

'Let me see,' said Melwyn who was consumed with curiosity but couldn't see the map as the other two were in the way. Jory reluctantly handed the map over to Melwyn.

'If that's where we are there's a dotted line from here that goes over to the other side of the island.' she said. 'Do you think that's a way across? And there's a little drawing that looks like a cave or a hole or something.'

Jory took the map back off her and studied it again. 'You could be right,' and he looked along the beach and up at the cliffs.

'Well don't let's just stand here,' Melwyn exclaimed, 'let's go and look,' and she started striding across the sand towards the bottom of the cliffs.

Jory and Mazy followed after Melwyn who had stopped and was staring up at the top of the cliff. 'There's a sort of a gap up there,' she said.

They continued to clamber over seaweed covered rocks and splash through rock pools towards the back of the beach.

'The tide comes right up here,' observed Jory. 'We'd better find a way off soon.'

Mazy looked back at the sea and saw that it was quickly rushing up the beach. Where they had been standing was already covered in water. She looked back at the cliff and saw a small gap behind a large rock. She squeezed around the rock and saw a cave-like opening that went deep into the cliff face. It looked like someone had cut down through the cliff with a large knife. 'Over here,' she shouted. 'There's a narrow pathway that climbs up the cliff.'

Jory and Melwyn appeared from behind the rock and looked at the deep opening. Mazy pointed to a small but well-defined path that made its way up inside the rocky crack.

Jory held up the map and looked at it closely in the sunlight. 'That must be the dotted line here. It looks like it will take us to the top of the cliff.'

'But will it take us to the rest of the crew?' asked Melwyn trying to look at the map at the same time.

'I don't know,' replied Jory rolling up the map and stuffing it into his pocket, 'but it's the only way up so I say we try it and see if we can find the others. The map doesn't show the island as being particularly big so it shouldn't take long.'

'But what about Ralph the Wrath? I don't want to find him. He might eat us. Can't we just go back to the boat and save ourselves?' pleaded Melwyn.

'Never!' exclaimed Mazy fiercely, 'My uncle saved our lives on the ship and gave us the boat to escape in. I'm not going to leave him now, not if there's any chance of saving him and the rest of the crew.' She turned away from Melwyn not waiting for an answer and began to climb the path up between the sheer cliffs. She was angry with Melwyn suggesting they run away. She's such a coward she thought. I don't know why she's my friend. The path was narrow and made up of small loose stones that shifted and skittered under her feet. She supported herself with both hands on the sides of the cliff and stepped purposefully upwards. She could hear stones being dislodged behind her so she knew at least Jory was following her. She secretly hoped Melwyn would come as well. Seagulls flew around her in big dizzy circles screaming 'Go Back, Go Back.' or that's what it sounded like to her. I'll call seagulls Melwyn in future she thought to herself.

The pathway ended at a flat-sided rock but the cliff rose

still higher above Mazy's head.

'Come to the end of the track?' said Jory breathlessly behind her.

'Yes.' She looked back the way they had come. 'What happened to Melwyn?'

'Don't worry, she's coming.' He stared up at the rock blocking their way. 'Move out of the way, I think I could climb up and see if the path carries on any further.'

Mazy squashed herself against the cliff face on one side and watched Jory climb up the rock and disappear over the top.

'Anything there?' called out Mazy straining to see over the top. There was no answer, just the sound of rattling stones as Melwyn arrived, red in the face and panting.

'Sorry, I'm a bit slow,' she said. 'Where's Jory?'

Jory's face appeared at the top of the rock. 'Up here. There is a way. Actually, there's two ways which is going to be a problem. Why don't I help you up and you can see for yourself.' He lay down on the top of the rock and stretched his arm down towards Mazy. 'Here hold on to me and I'll help you up.'

Mazy reached up and held onto Jory's hand. She scrabbled with her boots and scraped her knees as Jory heaved her up and helped her scramble over the top.

'Ouch,' she said rubbing her knees. 'That's going to sting.' She looked around and saw a cliff face that completely blocked any further progress. 'You said there was a way?' she said to Jory.

'Hang on,' he replied as he helped pull Melwyn up to

join them. 'Come with me.'

Mazy and Melwyn followed Jory around more rocks until they came to two cave entrances. 'That's what I meant about a way but it's a problem because there's two of them and they're both dark so I don't know which way to go or how we can see where we're going.'

'You mean I've climbed all the way up and now I've got to go all the way back down again?' complained Melwyn.

Mazy ignored her. Mazy didn't like the idea of them splitting up although she thought that if they did she would make sure Melwyn went into the darkest cave on her own.

'What do you think we should do Mazy?' asked Jory.

For once in her life, Mazy didn't know what to do. She looked around her hoping to see another way. She saw a seagull looking at her. 'Well, which way Mr Seagull?' she said.

'Left.'

Mazy stared at the seagull. 'Did that seagull just talk?' she said.

'Don't be daft Mazy,' replied Jory, 'birds don't talk. Don't know why you're asking him.'

'Cause he's the most sensible thing around here,' she muttered.

'Just a minute,' interrupted Melwyn.

'What is it now? You want to go back I suppose. Runaway; leave everyone who helped us to their fate, being eaten alive.' shouted Mazy.

'Wait,' said Melwyn ignoring Mazy's angry outburst.

'It wasn't the seagull; it came from one of the caves.'

Mazy stared hard at her friend. 'I'm the crazy one, Crazy Mazy that's what they call me but now you're hearing a cave speak. Have to call you crazy, crazy cowardly Melwyn from now on.'

'I am not crazy, and I'm not a coward. I'm here, aren't I? And I heard the cave speak.'

'You're not a coward,' interrupted Jory trying to make some peace between them. 'But you have to agree with Mazy that caves don't talk.'

Mazy glared at her friend and Melwyn glared back.

'Left.'

There was complete silence. No one said a word.

'You did hear it, didn't you,' insisted Melwyn.

'That's not possible,' said Jory walking towards the cave entrance.

Mazy and Melwyn joined him. 'Maybe there's magic here,' said Melwyn. 'There's magic out on the moors.'

They stood in complete silence staring into the blackness of the cave. Mazy squeezed Melwyn's hand. 'Sorry,' she whispered.

'That's all right,' acknowledged Melwyn and squeezed Mazy's hand back.

Mazy could feel her heart thumping in her chest. A cold breeze blew across her face, from inside the mouth of the cave and Mazy shivered. She could hear the waves crashing far below them and the occasional call from a seagull. Inside the cave it was completely quiet.

'Hello?' shouted Jory which made Mazy jump.

There was no reply.

'This *is* crazy,' said Jory, 'talking to a cave.'

'But we all heard it,' said Mazy.

'Hello cave,' shouted Jory.

The reply, when it came, was unmistakable. Screeching back from the darkness was a parrot's shriek, 'Left a bit!'

'It's Left a Bit,' exclaimed Mazy.

Chapter Eleven

Passages, caves and keys.

Jory stepped into the entrance of the cave. Mazy followed him and took his hand. 'Come on Melwyn,' she said.

Melwyn took Mazy's hand and the three of them entered the cave. Mazy peered into the darkness ahead of them. She felt a drip of water fall onto her neck. 'I can't see anything,' she said.

Jory stumbled over the uneven ground as he slid his hand along the rock wall of the cave to help guide him.

'Are you sure this is a good idea?' whispered Melwyn.

Mazy wasn't too sure either. 'Jory, how are we going to find the way inside?' she said, tugging on his hand.

Jory stopped and stared into the dark tunnel ahead of them. 'I think I can see some light ahead.'

Mazy pushed past him and stared. She could make out a sliver of light, 'You're right,' she said, 'come on,' and she dragged Jory and Melwyn further into the cave.

They stumbled over hidden objects and scraped their hands on the sharp rocks as they felt their way through the cave towards the light. The light flickered, throwing moving shadows along the cave wall as though there were monsters ahead waiting for them.

'Left a bit,' called out Mazy.

'Left a bit!' was the shrieking reply.

'Who's there,' sounded another voice.

'That sounded like Mr Fizz,' exclaimed Melwyn. 'I think we've found them.'

Mazy stepped into the light and found herself in a large cavern which stretched up high above her and away in all directions. On the opposite side light flooded in through an entrance. In the centre was a small fire and in the glow, she could see the shadowy shapes of the crew from The Black Booger.

A dishevelled Mr Fizz stood up and looked in her direction, 'Miss Mazy, is that you?'

Other crew members slowly came to their feet and looked at Mazy. She quickly checked to see if they were all present. There was Mr Fizz she had already seen and there was Sam and Dave. There was Skirtle and Gruntle and Mr Lost.

All the crew started talking at once. 'How did you get here?' 'We thought you had drowned.' 'Drowned.' 'Are we glad to see you.' 'Have you seen the captain?'

'Captain?' inquired Mazy. 'Isn't he with you?'

'Haven't seen him.' said Dave.

'Seen him,' said Sam.

'Is that young Jory with you as well?' asked Mr Fizz as Jory stepped forward.

'Yes I'm here,' replied Jory.

'And I'm here too,' squeaked Melwyn.

'Well, well well,' gasped Mr Fizz. 'And how did you manage to find us?'

Jory started to say, 'We found a....' but Mazy kicked him hard on his shin. 'We just thought we'd look for you and here we are,' she said.

Jory glared at her and rubbed his leg. 'Why did you do that?' he hissed.

'Don't tell them there's a map of the island.' Mazy whispered. 'They'll want to see it and when they see the word gold we'll never get away.'

'Why haven't you escaped?' asked Melwyn.

'We're all locked up,' said Dave. He lifted his arm and showed them a manacle around his wrist attached to a length of rusty chain.

'Locked up,' said Sam.

'We thought Ralph the giant would have eaten you by now.' said Melwyn.

'Well we thought he would too,' replied Skirtle, 'but he tipped us in here and locked us up and he's disappeared.'

'Was my uncle with you when you were brought in?' asked Mazy.

'Oh yes, the captain was with us but Ralphie he took the captain away with him. I don't think he was going to eat him because we could hear the captain laughing. You don't laugh if you're about to be eaten, do you? Anyways we ain't seen the captain since.'

'I hope the captain does get eaten,' muttered Mr Lost who was still sat on the ground.

'Don't be like that,' said Gruntle. 'He is the captain.'

'That's a horrible thing to say,' said Mazy. 'Why would you say that?'

'Because he got us in this mess, him and his treasure map. I tried to tell him it was a fake but he wouldn't listen. Anyway, I was proved right. This island doesn't look a bit like the map and here we are trapped and about to get eaten or worse.'

Sam looked worried, 'What's worse than being eaten?'

'Don't worry Sam,' said Jory lifting a chain and examining it closely. 'We're going to get you out of here before then.' Jory dropped the chain and began searching the cavern for anything that might help.

Water dripped from the roof of the cavern and the walls were covered in a green slime. Jory stepped over piles of rocks and mouldy mud as he searched the floor of the cave. In one corner he saw something sticking out of the ground. He reached down and pulled it out. It made a sucking sound as he pulled on it and with a shout he dropped it again.

'You ok?' called Mazy who was searching on the other side of the cavern.

'Yes, I'm fine,' Jory called back but he was shaking as

he pushed the human bone away with his foot. He
decided it would be better not to tell any of the others
that it looked like Ralph the Wrath did eat his prisoners
after all.

Melwyn watched Jory searching at the edge of the cave.
The firelight gave him a huge shadow which twisted
and curved like a giant spider crawling along but out of
sight. A drip of water, which fell from the roof, landed
on her face and made her jump. The sun shining
through the cave entrance looked like a nicer place to
go. Outside she felt the warmth of the sun on her face
and a soft breeze on her face. That's better she thought
but she did wonder how on earth they were going to
escape from the island. It all seemed such an enormous
problem. It was just one thing after another that had
started with that stupid cat. Melwyn walked a little way
from the cave entrance and sat down on a large rock. In

front of her was a gentle grass slope which was covered in sunflowers. Beyond that was a stone wall with small trees growing out of it and beyond that she could make out the sea. It all seemed so peaceful. I wish it could stay like this forever she thought. She gave out a sigh and sliding down off the rock she turned back towards the cavern entrance and stopped in surprise. On the outside of the opening was a tall tree and hanging on one of the branches was a rusty looking ring and hanging from the ring was a bunch of keys. There were no branches to climb up and the keys were too high for her to reach. She looked around for something she could use to reach them but there was nothing. Perhaps Jory would have an idea. She returned to the cavern and peered in. She couldn't see Jory but did see Mazy who was in conversation with Mr Fizz.

'Mazy,' she called out. 'Is Jory there?'

Mazy looked in her direction and shouted back, 'Oh there you are. I thought you'd run away and left us. Don't suppose you could help us out or is that too much for you?'

Melwyn stared at her friend.

'Well?' continued Mazy in a loud voice so everyone could hear. 'Or would you rather go outside and lie in the sun?'

Melwyn didn't know what to say. She wanted to say she had found some keys which may be the ones they needed. She wanted to ask for help in retrieving them but instead she turned on her heel and stamped out of the cavern. Over her head clattered the captain's parrot, Left a Bit. Melwyn turned right out of the cavern entrance and looked up at the keys on the ring above her head and out of reach. She grimaced in thought. She glanced around her and saw a small pile of rocks. She collected a handful and put them in her pocket to carry them closer to the base of the tree. Taking one of the rocks from her pocket she heaved it as hard as she could up towards the keys. The stone flew up and crashed through the branches showering leaves down on Melwyn. Oh no, she thought as she realised the stone was on its return path. She jumped away from the falling stone just in time to see it fly past her head and bounce along the ground. Left a Bit was watching her closely.

'I think I should move a bit further away, don't you,' she said to the parrot whilst brushing the leaves off her head. She stepped away from the tree and to one side. Taking another stone from her pocket she squinted with her eyes and threw the stone as hard as she could towards the keys. The stone struck the keyring and flew away out of sight. Melwyn held her breath as she watched the keys bounce in the tree. The keys stayed where they were.

'Drat!' she said and took another stone from her pocket. The parrot flew closer to her and screeched, 'Left a bit.'

'You could well be right,' answered Melwyn and taking careful aim, hurled the stone. This time it hit the keys so hard they spun off the branch and tumbled down to the ground. Melwyn snatched them up gleefully and ran back to the cave.

'I've found the keys,' she shouted. 'I haven't been wasting my time.'

Everyone in the cave looked up in astonishment. Mr Fizz was the first to speak. 'How on earth did you find those?' he asked looking at her wide-eyed.

'They were on a tree outside,' she explained, enjoying the look on Mazy's face. 'They were high up but I managed to knock them off with a rock.'

Jory splashed through the water to her. Melwyn handed him the keys and he turned back towards the manacled crew.

'Fantastic,' exclaimed Mr Fizz, standing up as Jory approached him.

'You're a genius,' said Dave.

'Genius,' said Sam.

All of the crew huddled around Mr Fizz as Jory tried the key in the locks on his wrist.

Mazy walked across to Melwyn. 'That was clever,' she said apologetically. 'Thank you.'

'It works!' Jory exclaimed.

In a few minutes, Jory had released all the crew from their manacles. The men stood around rubbing their wrists and talking excitedly about being free. 'What now?' inquired Mr Lost. 'We're still stuck on the island with no hope of escape and that giant's certain to come back and capture us again.'

'But there is an escape,' shouted Mazy. 'We found a ship washed up on the beach. I'm sure with a high tide and all of us pulling and pushing we could get it back into the sea.'

'A ship, you say,' said Mr Fizz not believing their good luck. 'What sort of ship?'

'It's a bit smaller than The Black Booger,' said Melwyn. 'It's called The Scarlet Arrow. Have you heard of it?'

There was dead silence in the cave. It was as if time stood still. A chill wind blew from the outside and Mazy shivered. There's something we don't know she thought. Something terrible has happened in the past.

'What do you know about The Scarlet Arrow?' she asked no one in particular.

No one replied. There was a shuffling of feet and the crew avoided looking at her face. It was Gruntle who broke the silence.

'Well you see, Miss Mazy,' he began picking his words carefully. 'We do know about The Scarlett Arrow but we all thought she had been lost some time ago. So it was a bit of a surprise to us that you found her, that's all.'

'No, that's not all, Gruntle.' said Mazy firmly. 'The Black Booger was supposed to have been The Scarlet Arrow and my uncle was supposed to have renamed her and there was supposed to be another fearsome pirate named Jehoshaphat the Terrible.'

'Well,' continued Gruntle, 'there was another Pirate and maybe there was another ship but it was a long time ago and I don't think any of that is interesting stuff anymore.'

'Well it is to me,' said Mazy.

'I don't want to be a wet blanket over this fascinating history lesson,' interrupted Mr Lost, 'but don't you think our time would be better spent escaping.' He made the word 'escaping' very loud.

Dave and Sam started to move towards the back of the

cave. 'You came in here, didn't you?' he said to Jory. 'So this must be the way out.'

'Way out,' said Sam.

The rest of the crew followed as Dave disappeared into the dark passageway at the back of the cavern. Melwyn grabbed hold of Sam's hand and followed him closely.

'Just a minute,' shouted Mazy. 'Haven't we forgotten someone?'

Gruntle bumped into the back of Mr Fizz who had stopped at Mazy's question. 'Keep going,' he hissed. 'There's no one.'

Gruntle reluctantly turned around knowing full well to whom Mazy was referring. 'You meaning the captain?' he said.

'Of course I mean the captain. He's still somewhere on

the island and we have to rescue him too.'

'Well,' began Gruntle. 'I think you may have to settle on the fact that the captain is, well, he's possibly not on the island anymore, in a manner of speaking.'

Dave had reappeared with Sam and followed by Melwyn. Dave was nodding his head as if in agreement. 'The captain is gone, Mistress Mazy. I'm sorry that he is but the last we seen of him was being taken off by Ralph the Wrath. And we all know what Ralph does to his prisoners.'

'We don't know that for certain,' said Jory.

Sam nodded but his face was screwed up in a grimace. He put his head on one side and finally said, 'Captain's captain, he'd look out for us.' Jory nodded in agreement.

Melwyn looked at Gruntle and Sam and thought if she didn't say something they would never escape. The idea of being eaten did not appeal to her. Her stomach rumbled and reminded her that she was also hungry, which almost certainly meant Ralph the Wrath was hungry too.

'And while we looking out for the captain, who's most certainly dead,' she said, 'we will all get caught again and there'll not be anyone else to come to our rescue. We need to escape out of here.' She turned to set off towards the back of the cavern again.

'I think she's right,' agreed Dave and began to follow her.

The rest of the crew hesitantly turned away from Mazy, except Sam and Jory.

Mazy jumped up onto a rock and looked down on the retreating crew. 'Just a minute,' she shouted, 'Who came and rescued you? Who could have sailed away and left you to be eaten? Who found a way to unlock you? It was us, Jory, Melwyn and me. We didn't leave you to die but we could have done. You owe us and my uncle, at least to see if he's still alive and see if we can rescue him.'

Sam grabbed Dave's arm, 'She's right. We have to rescue the captain.'

Dave's shoulders slumped. 'Ok,' he agreed, 'but as soon as we find out he's a goner we're out of here, agreed?'

'Agreed,' replied Mazy her eyes shining with excitement. She jumped down from her rock and headed towards the cavern entrance and out into the sunshine. Her heart was thumping in her chest and her legs felt wobbly but she was elated. They're following me! I'm the new temporary captain. Her uncle was alive, she just knew it. This adventure wasn't over yet.

Right at the back Melwyn scowled. 'You'll all be eaten,' she called out but no one took any notice of her as they trooped after Mazy, the 'Temporary Captain' if only in her mind.

Chapter Twelve

'He's not a chicken.'

They walked along a narrow pathway which led away from the cavern and down towards a low stone wall. Mazy followed the path in the absence of any other ideas. Jory walked alongside her. He pointed ahead of them, 'It looks like there may be a view over the wall. The island isn't that big and we might possibly see the whole of that side.'

They walked on through grass that grew taller and taller as they approached the wall. The yellow flowers that had been dotted about all over the field had given way to some nasty looking weeds which grew up and out of the stones in front of them. The wall was covered in tangled ivy and made up of broken and jagged stones all along its length. 'Let me help you up,' offered Jory and held out his hand to Mazy. She scrambled up on top of the wall and shielded her eyes from the sun. She saw a long valley which stretched away down to the sea.

'What can you see?' asked Mr Lost.

'I can see the sea. It's not too far away. Down to the left I can see some smoke rising and a huge wooden building like it might be the giant's house. Oh, hang on I can see the top of Ralph's head moving about.'

'Can you see the captain?' called up Gruntle.

Mazy stood up on tiptoe, 'Not yet, but if he's down there I won't be able to see him from here.'

'Any ideas how to get closer without being seen?' asked Jory.

Mazy looked at the land ahead where they would all

have to cross. There were trees and large rocks which would provide some cover. Beyond that was a narrow gulley which disappeared over the cliff edge near where she had seen the top of Ralph's head.

She turned around and held out her hand. 'Help me down.'

Mazy climbed off the wall helped by Jory and Gruntle. The other members of the crew looked at her expectantly.

'There is a way,' she began, 'if we go left a bit from here.'

She was interrupted by her Uncle's parrot screaming 'LEFT A BIT, LEFT A BIT' at the top of its voice.

'Can someone keep that parrot quiet,' snarled Mr Fizz.

'Never did like the stupid bird,' he muttered as Sam

cradled Left a Bit in his arms and shushed it to be quiet.

Mazy continued, 'As I was saying if we go to that side,' she waved her hand to indicate left, 'and use the trees and rocks to cover ourselves I think we will be able to get closer. There is a gulley there which I am hoping we can fit inside and get close to where I think Ralph is.'

'I don't like the sound of smoke,' said Gruntle. 'Could be he's already eaten the Captain and will be looking for us next.'

'That's right,' exclaimed Melwyn, pushing forward. 'This is stupid; going towards a giant who we know will eat us instead of running away. I say we should go back to the cavern and make our way back to the beach.'

Gruntle and Dave were nodding their heads in

agreement. Mazy knew that she had to take immediate charge if she was going to persuade the crew to help save her uncle.

She raised herself up as tall as she could and in a commanding tone gave her orders, 'My uncle, the captain of The Black Booger, is in danger. I am his niece and I have taken temporary command of The Black Booger in his absence. I am now your captain and you will do what I say.'

'What?' shrieked Melwyn. 'You?'

Mazy looked at the other members of the crew wondering if she had tried too hard.

'S'right,' said Sam ignoring Melwyn. 'I'm with Captain Mazy of The Black Booger.' And he stood next to Mazy and stared at his crewmates. Jory stood on the other side of Mazy to lend her his support.

Mr Lost was first to speak. 'Well, this is a bit irregular considering the captain hated women on his ship, never mind one in charge but I will stand with you Mazy. At least we should see if the captain is alive and take it from there.'

Mazy breathed a silent sigh of relief. Ignoring the rest of the crew and whatever they may have thought Mazy turned to her left and said, 'Right then, lets us go and rescue our captain.' She walked away, hoping they would all follow her, which they all did except Melwyn.

Melwyn wasn't taken in at all by her friend's posturing. 'Well I'm not coming with you,' she shouted out defiantly. 'I think you're all completely mad.' And she sat down on the broken wall and wondered what she was going to do next.

The ground beyond the wall was rough and uneven with large tusks of grass and rocks, Mazy stepped carefully around the rocks and headed towards a large tree, keeping it between her and where she had last seen Ralph the Wrath. The rest of the crew followed silently behind her in a single file. Sam held onto Left a Bit to keep it quiet and they all arrived at the tree without being seen.

'What now, captain?' asked Sam.

Mazy beamed at him. He had been the most supportive of all of them.

'We need to scout out our route ahead before we go any

further.' she replied.

Dave and Mr Lost were peering around the side of the tree and Dave responded over his shoulder, 'You were right about the gulley. It's quite deep and it looks as though it goes all the way to the edge of the cliff. That's where the smoke is coming from too. Looks pretty tricky but I think someone could crawl along it and have a look-see.'

Mazy joined them and looked at the gulley herself. 'Can't we all go?' she asked not liking the idea of splitting up.

'We could,' Dave replied, 'but if we're spotted we're all in for it. If only one of us goes and gets caught the rest of you have a better chance of getting away.'

'You said 'the rest of you', does that mean you're

volunteering?' asked Mazy.

'Yeah, I'll go. You lot stay here. I'll wave if it's safe to join me,' and he lowered himself down to his hands and knees and began crawling towards the gulley.

A loud crash came from below the cliff edge making everyone jump. A huge shower of bright orange sparks shot skywards together with great plumes of white smoke.

Dave looked back over his shoulder, 'Looks like he's getting the fire good and ready for me,' he whispered. 'Let's hope I give him indigestion.' And giving a wink he was gone into the gulley and out of sight. Mazy watched the gulley impatiently waiting for a sign. 'I should have gone,' she said quietly to Jory who was stood next to her. 'I'm the captain.'

'We need you here to lead us,' replied Jory. 'No point losing two captains in one trip. Wouldn't look good, would it?'

Mazy smiled at him. Although she had no idea what she was going to do and her heart was pounding in her chest and her palms were all sweaty she knew she could rely on Jory. She wondered if he resented her being in charge but the thought vanished from her mind as she saw a hand rise up from the gulley and wave at them.

'Come on,' she said in a whisper. She dropped down on her hands and knees and crawled towards the gulley followed by Jory and the rest.

The gulley was filled with stones and weeds and stinging nettles. Spider's webs clung to the tall grasses which grew from the top edges of the gulley. There were small puddles of water turning the earth to mud.

By the time Mazy joined up with Dave her hands were covered in mud and her face was covered in spider's web. Mazy wiped the spider's webs from her face and eyes but in doing so wiped mud all around her face.

Dave looked around at her approach. 'You come in disguise?'

Mazy ignored him, 'What can you see?'

'A bit further up ahead I could see down over the cliff edge. There are grassy mounds which lead onto the beach and Ralph is stoking a huge fire and there's a big cooking pot hung over it so I think he's getting ready for cooking his dinner.'

Mazy's stomach gurgled and she realised just how hungry she was. 'Did you see my uncle?'

'Oh yeah, he's down there all right. Trussed up like a

chicken, which is what Ralph probably sees him as.'

'What's he say?' whispered Sam hoarsely from the back.

'Captain's been turned into a chicken,' came the reply.

'Cripes,' muttered Sam, 'that's terrible strong magic to do that.'

Mazy smiled grimly to herself and thought they could do with some terrible strong magic of their own if they were going to rescue her uncle.

'Any ideas?' she asked Dave who was peering over the edge of the cliff.

Dave scratched his head and frowned, 'I don't know, maybe if we could cause some kind of diversion so Ralph looks another way we could sneak down behind his back and onto the beach.'

A flapping and squawking came from behind Mazy.
'Can't you be quiet?' she said.

Sam was trying to hold onto Left a Bit and had his
hands well and truly full trying to control the parrot.

Mazy turned back to Dave, 'What sort of diversion?'
but his reply was interrupted by a shriek and a squawk
as Left a Bit finally broke free from Sam's clawing
hands. It raced away, flapping its wings furiously and
headed for the beach screaming 'LEFT A BIT, LEFT A
BIT' at the top of its voice.

The parrot flew straight for the Giant's head and
flapped and squawked at him, diving at his face and
veering away at the last moment. Ralph the Wrath flung
his arms around his head trying to knock the parrot out
of the sky. Again and again, Left a Bit attacked Ralph.

'That parrot's gone crazy,' said Sam looking over Mazy's shoulder.

Dave scrambled to his feet and shouted, 'Come on, now's our chance.' He ran bent over to the edge of the cliff and skidded down its sloping face on the seat of his trousers. Mazy jumped up right behind him, followed by Jory and the rest of the crew. Some slid down the cliff, some rolled down and Sam, who tripped at the top, bounced down on his head until they were all at the bottom.

'Ralph's still busy,' whispered Jory.

Ralph had taken up a huge wooden cudgel and was swinging it around his head in huge circles trying to swat Left a Bit who was squawking at the top of its voice.

'All the time we can hear Left a Bit we know Ralph's occupied,' said Mazy. 'Let' go.'

She led the men across the grassy hillocks towards the beach. 'Spread out a bit,' she instructed, 'and look for the captain, he's tied up somewhere.'

Mazy and Jory headed towards the huge fire which was sending its sparks spiralling up into the sky. Dave and Sam went off to the left and the rest went off to the right. They could still hear Ralph the Wrath bellowing in the distance, occasionally interrupted by the squawking of Left a Bit.

The smoke from the fire was being blown around in great gusts. Sometimes Mazy could see Dave and Sam and sometimes they disappeared behind the dense white smoke. When the smoke blew in her direction it made her throat sting and her eyes became watery. Jory was a shadowy figure ahead of her as they headed towards the sea.

She heard Jory shout, 'I can see him'.

The smoke cleared and Mazy ran after Jory. He was heading towards what looked like a pile of old clothes lying on the ground. Mazy caught up with him and saw the pile of clothes was her uncle, Captain Blind Lightning Henry. He was tied from head to foot. Dave and Sam ran over to join them.

'He's not a chicken,' said Sam sounding a little disappointed.

'What are you doing here?' croaked the captain staring wildly at them in disbelief.

'We've come to rescue you,' replied Mazy. She looked at Dave, 'Have you got a knife to cut him free?'

Dave produced a long thin knife from his trouser pocket and started to cut the ropes around the captain. Mazy feverishly pulled at the ends until her uncle was untied.

'You're all blistering crazy, coming back for me. You should have escaped when you had the chance.'

Sam scratched the side of his cheek, 'You could have just said thank you.'

'Well of course,' blustered Blind Lightning Henry wobbling on his feet, 'I didn't mean it like that. But what in blinding barnacles are you doing here Mazy? I thought I told you and Jory and that Melwyn girl to escape in the rowing boat.'

'Well we didn't,' said Mazy. She was beginning to think her uncle was being incredibly ungrateful considering the danger that they were all in.

'Come on captain,' said Dave and lifted Blind Lightning Henry to his feet.

'Legs a bit wonky,' the rescued captain muttered as he staggered along the beach supported by Dave and Sam. 'Don't seem to want to go in my direction.'

Mazy looked around to see if she could alert the rest of the crew they were leaving with her uncle. With a huge feeling of relief she saw Mr Lost, and Mr Fizz and Skirtle running in their direction.

'Where's Gruntle?' she asked them as they arrived panting and out of breath.

'I don't know, replied Mr Fizz. 'He went off saying something about finding some food as he was feeling hungry.'

Mazy scanned the beach but there was no sign of the

cook. She heard Jory call to her so she turned and ran. They all headed back towards the sloping cliff to retrace their steps.

Dave and Sam were supporting the captain on each side as he seemed unable to walk.

'How are we getting off the island?' Mazy heard him say.

'Got a boat, captain, don't you worry,' replied Dave, 'just need to drag you up this cliff and we'll be gone.'

Jory looked at Mazy and said, 'I can't hear Left a Bit any more. You don't suppose Ralph got him in the end?'

In answer to Jory's question there came a great howl from behind them. They all stopped to look back and saw Ralph the Wrath holding a huge wooden club in his hand. He was waving it over his head and bellowing like an angry bull. Mazy's legs turned to jelly and her stomach froze tight as she watched the giant swing his club down with great force into the fire. Burning logs and sparks and smoke burst away in all directions.

'Run!' screamed Mazy but as they all turned and ran as fast as they could, Mazy knew they would never make it.

Chapter Thirteen

The Rescue.

The stone wall was sharp and uneven. Melwyn fidgeted around trying to find a more comfortable place to sit. She looked at the seagulls in the distance and tried to count them but there were too many and they flew and dodged around each other. She looked out across the field and wondered if someone had planted the flowers. She examined her nails and tried to clean them. Finally, she thought about Mazy and Jory and the rest of the crew.

Why were they so stupid? Why would they go and get themselves eaten for no good purpose? They could have been off the island ages ago. Mazy's uncle had got them into this mess in the first place. He was so dumb following a fake treasure map. He deserves to be eaten but not us as well. Now I'm completely stuck here.

Melwyn sighed. She kicked a rock with her foot and turned towards the gulley where she had last seen her friends. Far away there was a sound like an angry parrot. Slowly she headed out from under the tree towards the cliff edge which she could see some distance away. I suppose I'd better go and see what's going on.

The gulley looked wet and muddy with stinging nettles so she walked along the edge. She could still hear the parrot squawking but the sound was from further away. The edge of the cliff was becoming closer and she could smell wood smoke and see occasional sparks flying up into the sky. They're all probably dead, she thought. No point on carrying on. Better go back and see if I can get away in the rowing boat. However, Melwyn's legs had other ideas and they remorselessly carried her further and further towards the edge of the cliff.

When she arrived at the cliff top she saw the top of Ralph the Wrath's head moving towards the beach on her left. She ducked down so she couldn't be seen and heard the most awful howl of rage followed by a huge crash. She looked up and saw sparks and smoke billowing up into the sky and Ralph the Wrath waving a huge club around over his head. The giant wasn't looking at her so she ran towards the edge of the cliff to see what was going on. She threw her hand over her mouth as she saw Mazy and Jory and the rest of the crew on the beach. Ralph the Wrath was shouting and lumbering towards them. She heard Mazy scream and they all turned and ran towards the cliff.

Melwyn ran along the cliff edge towards her friends screaming at the top of her voice. 'RUN, RUN.'

It was pointless. In a few strides Ralph the Wrath would catch up with them.

Melwyn stopped and gazed in mounting horror as she realised her friends would be caught and eaten. There must be something, she thought. There must be something. She thrust her hands into her pockets in desperation, searching for anything that could help. Rocks, she still had some rocks from when she knocked the key down from the tree. She dragged one out from her pocket and threw it as hard as she could, straight at Ralph' head. It went far too high. Ralph was almost upon her friends. Melwyn took a deep breath and took another stone from her pocket. Ralph was bending down towards Mazy. He had his huge hand outstretched to grab her when Melwyn launched her stone. It flew through the smoky air and bounced off the side of Ralph's knobbly nose. Ralph snatched his hand away from Mazy and clutched at his bleeding nose.

'OWWWW.' He cried out and sat down heavily on his bottom with both hands wrapped around his nose. 'That hurts.'

'Come on,' shouted Melwyn and waved her arms furiously at Mazy and the others.

Mazy looked up at the top of the cliff and couldn't believe her eyes. She could see Melwyn waving her arms and shouting at them to run.

Dave and Sam had already started running, dragging the captain along with them. Jory grabbed Mazy's hand, 'Come on Mazy, it's our chance to escape.'

'But what about Gruntle?' she panted.

Jory pointed behind her, 'Look he's coming.'

Mazy looked around and saw Gruntle running towards them as fast as his legs could take him, which wasn't very fast because he was carrying a large sack over his shoulders.

'Come on,' urged Jory and dragged Mazy along after the rest of the crew.

Ralph was still sitting on the ground holding his nose, shaking his head from side to side and moaning loudly.

'Cry baby,' muttered Mazy as she ran with Jory to the bottom of the cliff. Dave and Sam and Mr Fizz and Mr Lost and Skirtle were working together to pull and push the captain and themselves up the sloping face of the cliff. Gruntle caught them up, puffing and wheezing still with his large sack over his shoulder.

'What you got there, Gruntle,' asked Sam.

'Food,' he gasped. 'Going to be hungry soon.'

Mazy's stomach rumbled at the thought of food and she realised that none of them had eaten for some time. She scrambled up the cliff behind everyone else glad, they were all together. Even Melwyn was there. Mazy had seen her throwing rocks at Ralph and she threw her arms around her friend and said, 'Thank you,' over and over again.

'Time for that later,' said Dave hauling on the captain. 'We must get back to the cave and the passages you told us about before Ralph stops crying over his bleeding nose. And it's going to get dark soon.'

They ran and stumbled back across the field, the fading

light making it more and more difficult to see where to place their feet. Mazy gripped Melwyn's hand and they helped each other across the stones and grassy mounds. There was no sound of Ralph following them and they soon arrived at the cavern where the crew had been held prisoner. It was pitch dark inside but Mr Lost produced a flint and using it against a stone he was able to make a spark. He grabbed a dried-up branch and set fire to the end. 'Follow me,' he said and holding the lit branch above his head, he led the way to the back of the cavern. They kept close to each other as they stumbled over rocks and splashed through puddles.

'Got two ways to go,' called out Mr Lost. 'Any ideas you three?'

'Go right,' shouted Jory from the back of the group. 'I'm sure we came in from that direction.'

'Righty ho,' replied Mr Lost and he headed down the dark, right-hand passage followed by the rest of the crew.

Each time they came to a fork it was Jory who remembered the way they had come, and so Mr Lost followed his directions.

Eventually Mazy heard him say, 'Bit of daylight ahead.' She could feel a cool breeze and heard a seagull mewing in the distance. They stood outside the entrance and looked down the gulley to the beach. The light was fading fast and it looked steeper than Mazy remembered. 'The ship is down there,' said Mazy. 'We've just got to climb down.'

'That little boat isn't going to take all of us,' said Mr Lost. 'Perhaps someone can take it and get some help.'

'No, not the small rowing boat,' explained Mazy.

'There's a ship on the beach big enough to take all of us. We need to get it into the sea.'

'A ship you say,' exclaimed Blind Lightning Henry, hauling himself up onto his feet. 'What sort of ship?'

'It's a sailing ship, smaller than The Black Booger and quite old but I'm sure it will sail.'

'It's called The Scarlet Arrow,' interrupted Melwyn.

Blind Lightning Henry lent forward and thrust his face right up to Melwyn's. His voice was hoarse, 'The Scarlet Arrow, never.'

Melwyn looked into his wild staring eyes. 'Yes,' she croaked.

No one said a word. Mazy looked at her uncle's wild staring eyes and shivered. He continued to stare into

Melwyn's face as though he didn't know what to do next. Dave pulled on his arm. 'Come on captain,' he said kindly, 'Let's get down from here before it gets too dark to see. Jory, you lead the way.'

Jory turned and lowered himself down from the ledge they were on and began to scramble down the gulley. Dave and Sam helped the captain down and they all followed on behind until they arrived at the beach. Jory stepped out from the cliff and pointed along the beach at a dark brooding shadow. 'There she is,' he said.

Mr Lost shook his head as he walked towards the ship. 'I don't believe it.' He looked back at Blind Lightning Henry who was being supported by Dave and Sam. 'You always wondered what happened and it looks like this is where she ended up.'

Blind Lightning Henry pushed Dave and Sam to one

side and staggered up to the side of the ship. He placed a hand on the hull and stared up at the masts above him. Mazy watched him in disbelief as her uncle's eyes filled with tears. The rest of the crew stood in a semi-circle around the captain and bowed their heads in silence.

'What's going on?' whispered Melwyn to Mazy.

'I don't know,' whispered Mazy back. 'There's something about this ship we don't know about.'

Mazy felt water sloshing over her feet.

'Scuse me for interrupting,' she said loudly, 'but the tide is coming in and it might be a good time to try and get the ship in the water if we can.'

Her uncle looked around at her. He wiped the back of his sleeve across his eyes, straightened up and commanded the crew.

'She's right. Let's see whether she's close enough and light enough for us to get her in the water. Dave, you and Sam start digging away at the sand in the front.'

The captain seemed to have recovered his strength and sense of purpose. 'You Jory, you go and help Dave and Sam. Mr Fizz you search the ship for any ropes that might be of use. With a decent high tide, we might yet float her off and make our escape under the cover of darkness.'

Mr Fizz climbed up into the ship and disappeared. He quickly reappeared with a handful of rope. 'Some here, captain.'

'Fasten it to the bow somewhere and throw the rest down to us.'

Mr Fizz disappeared again in the gloom and Mazy could hear him clattering along to the front of the ship. 'Below!' he shouted as he threw the rope down.

Dave, Sam and Jory were up to their knees in the sea. It had become impossible to shift any more sand away. The captain grabbed the end of the rope and waded out into the sea alongside Dave. He pointed to the rocks jutting up from the beach that weren't covered by the water yet. 'Up on there,' he said shoving Sam along. The waves were rolling in up the beach and Jory nearly lost his footing as he struggled to climb up onto a large rock. Dave shoved up on Jory's bottom, pushing him up onto the rock and climbed up himself. He was followed by the captain and Sam. The four of them took hold of the rope. 'Not yet,' said the captain. Wait until the tide's as high as it will get. The rest of you,' he shouted, 'get at the stern and when I shout give it a shove.'

Mazy, Melwyn, Gruntle, Mr Fizz, Skirtle and Mr Lost positioned themselves at the rear of The Scarlet Arrow and prepared themselves to push. The sea was running right up the beach, pushed by the incoming tide. Mazy heard a rumble of thunder in the distance. It was almost dark and she wondered if this was such a good idea. The water was still sloshing around her feet and up her ankles. 'Not long now,' said Mr Fizz. 'I think I can feel her getting jittery.'

Mazy could feel it too. The ship was rocking slightly with the action of the waves against the hull. Why doesn't he shout she thought? We'll drown if we don't start soon. The sea was splashing her up to her waist and tugging and pulling at her as if to take her out to sea. She hung onto the ship to stop herself from being knocked over. 'I'm scared,' whimpered Melwyn who was next to her and being thrown around by the waves.

'Hold steady,' said Mr Fizz. 'Any minute now and we'll be pushing hard. When we do and if she floats make sure you grab onto the ladder here at the back and climb up. We'll be trying to climb over you so you'd best go as fast as you can. Look out here she goes.'

Mazy felt the ship move and at the same time heard her uncle shouting at the top of his voice, 'PUSH, PUSH, PUSH.'

They all leant into the back of the ship and slipping and sliding about in the water they pushed as hard as they could. Mazy felt her feet slipping backwards in the sand and she nearly fell headlong into the sea. She steadied herself and pushed again. She could feel the ship moving. 'Up the ladder,' shouted Mr Fizz.

Mazy, who was closest, grabbed at the rope and pulled herself up onto the first rungs of the ladder. She heard a scream behind her and she looked back to see Melwyn

disappear under the water. Mr Lost dived into the

sloshing sea and disappeared too but he quickly came

back up to the surface dragging Melwyn with him.

'Go!' he shouted and Mazy scrambled up the swaying

ladder as fast as she could. She was quickly followed

by Mr Lost, Melwyn, Gruntle, Skirtle and finally Mr

Fizz. The ship was rocking from side to side as they

ran to the front of the ship. Lightning flashed down

from the dark sky and Mazy saw a dark figure climbing

over the edge of the deck. Her uncle, soaked through,

with seaweed hanging from his head, dragged himself

onto the ship. He was followed by a wet Sam.

'Where's Jory and Dave,' shouted Mazy.

'They're in the rowing boat, they're going to give us a

tow,' replied Sam wiping the seawater from his eyes

and face. He staggered as The Scarlett Arrow jolted forwards. 'I think we might have shifted her off,' he said and turned to lean over the front of the ship. Mazy joined him and peered into the dark. She could see the rowing boat ahead with two figures in it, pulling on two sets of oars. It looked so tiny almost hidden in the dark and the waves. 'They'll be all right?' she asked anxiously.

'Right as rain,' said her uncle cheerfully alongside her. 'Skirtle, run and see if there is anything resembling a sail we can use aloft.' There was another rumble of thunder but it sounded as though it was a long way away. 'Storm isn't going to bother us,' reassured the captain. 'I think there'll be some calmer weather very soon.'

Mazy continued to stare into the distance hoping to

catch sight of the little rowing boat. 'Please come back safely,' she whispered.

The Scarlet Arrow was clear of the rocks and wallowing up and down as it was slowly pulled further out to sea. The waves were beginning to drop away, smaller and smaller and the moon suddenly appeared from behind the clouds. Mazy traced her eye down the taught rope from the front of the ship and with a sudden lift in her stomach she spotted the rowing boat. She could make out Jory as he was a little smaller than Dave. They were both there still pulling on their oars. She heard a commotion behind her and she turned around to see Skirtle dragging a tangle of sailcloth along the deck.

'All hands on deck,' shouted her uncle and the crew surrounded the sail to untangle it. Skirtle, assisted by

Mr Lost, climbed up the mast dragging a rope behind him. 'High as you can,' ordered her uncle as Skirtle hung on to the slippery mast with both hands whilst holding onto the rope with his teeth. 'Arfule mufledum,' he shouted back. He wrapped his legs and one arm around the mast and lashed the rope around a peg jutting out from its centre. Sam and Gruntle grabbed the bottom corners of the sail and pulled each corner to opposite sides of the ship. The sail filled out with wind and Mazy felt The Scarlet Arrow rush forwards in a more purposeful manner. Skirtle came sliding down the mast and landed on the deck in a heap of arms and legs.

'Mr Lost, take the tiller,' commanded the captain.

'What about the other two?' Mazy shouted and ran to the front of the ship. She looked forward and saw The

Scarlet Arrow had almost caught up with the rowing boat. Dave and Jory had stopped rowing and were waving their arms frantically in the air. Her uncle joined her and with Gruntle the three of them began hauling on the rope attached to the boat. 'Get them alongside,' instructed the captain as the little rowing boat approached the side of the ship. Jory leant forward in the boat and took hold of the rope as it became vertical alongside The Scarlett Arrow's hull. He swung himself off the boat and placing his feet on the wooden side of the ship began to climb up. Dave was right behind him and the two of them tumbled over the side of the ship and collapsed onto the deck.

'Well done you two,' said the captain and marched away towards the rear of the ship.

Mazy knelt alongside Jory. 'Are you all right?'

Jory sat slumped over, leaning back against the side of the ship. His head was bent forward and he was panting. 'I'm so tired,' he said. 'My arms feel like they've been torn off, stitched back on and torn off again.'

Mazy put her arm around his shoulders, 'You did it though, I'm proud of you.'

Jory looked up at her and smiled a thin smile. 'Thank you Mazy. You've been brilliant too. If it wasn't for you we wouldn't all be together. Captain Mazy, eh?' and he nudged her with his elbow.

The Scarlet Arrow rolled and swayed as it slowly sailed further out to sea. Mazy looked over the side of the ship and watched the moonlight reflecting ghostly shapes across the surface of the waves. She looked back towards the island searching for any sign of a huge dark shadow that may be chasing after them but the island was lost in the darkness. Jory hauled himself up alongside her and touched her arm, 'Where's Melwyn?'

Mazy looked back along the ship and realised she hadn't seen her friend since they both climbed up the ladder. 'I don't know. I'll go and look for her.'

Mazy staggered along the rocking ship's deck and met Mr Fizz who was stumbling towards her. He was carrying two bowls which were steaming. Mazy smelt a delicious stewy sort of a smell. She smiled at Mr Fizz.

'Go see Gruntle,' he waved as he staggered past her and headed towards the front of the ship.

Chapter Fourteen

The secret of The Scarlet Arrow revealed.

Mazy climbed down the wooden ladder into the ship and found Gruntle stirring a large pot of bubbling stew over a fire. Her stomach tightened at the smell of the hot food. 'How did you manage that?' she asked.

'Well I knew you'd all be hungry once we escaped so when you were fighting old Ralph, I snuck into his house and stole some of his vegetables. Do you want some?'

Mazy sat down on a seat alongside a long bench. 'Yes please, but you knew we would escape?'

'Course.' Gruntle spooned out a generous helping of vegetable stew into a bowl in front of Mazy. 'Always escape, that's what us Pirates do. In, grab what we want, and escape in the nick of time.'

'But we were nearly killed,' slurped Mazy as she took a mouthful of hot stew.

'But we didn't,' insisted Gruntle and resumed stirring the pot of steaming vegetables.

Mazy blew on the spoonfuls of stew to cool them down and deciding to change the subject, she asked, 'Have you seen Melwyn?'

'I'm here,' said a voice from behind her.

Mazy turned around and saw her friend Melwyn holding some carrots.

'Drop them over here,' instructed Gruntle as he took up a large knife. 'They'll make a welcome addition to the stew.'

Melwyn dropped the carrots next to Gruntle who began to cut them up with great speed. She sat down on the bench next to Mazy and looked down at her hands in her lap as she twisted her fingers together.

Mazy examined her friend and saw her eyes were red and her face was pale. She placed a hand on Melwyn's arm, 'Are you all right?'

'I'm very tired. I've been helping Gruntle with the food but I feel like I want to sleep for a week.'

'It's been a busy day,' agreed Mazy trying to comfort her friend.

'Busy?' exclaimed Melwyn. 'We were nearly thrown overboard by your mad Uncle. We've been shipwrecked, nearly eaten by a giant, chased by a giant, ran till my legs felt like jelly, pushed a ship off the sand

and nearly drowned and I've been terrified the whole time. Yes, Mazy it's been very busy and I'm tired of all this I want to go home.'

'I'm sorry it turned out the way it did Melwyn, I truly am.'

'I'm sorry too Mazy. I don't mean to be angry but I haven't enjoyed this one bit.'

Gruntle looked up from chopping the carrots and waving the knife in their direction said, 'You two oughter to get some sleep. Long trip home and you both look like your dead on your feet or in your case your bottom.'

Melwyn slid off the bench and lay down on the floor. She tucked herself into a ball and almost instantly went to sleep.

'Brave girl, that,' said Gruntle and went back to cutting the carrots.

'Where's my uncle?' Mazy asked.

'The captain? He's in the cabin up ahead.'

Mazy ducked under swinging ropes and stepped over empty wooden boxes as she made her way towards the small cabin and knocked on the door.

'Go Away,' shouted her uncle in reply.

Mazy took no notice and pushed the door open. There was a lamp hanging from the ceiling. It was swinging from side to side and shadows danced around the walls. Her uncle was sat behind the desk with an empty bowl sliding backwards and forwards in front of him. It looked like it had been a bowl of stew. He was shuffling through a pile of dirty and torn papers. They looked like the ones that Mazy had seen when she searched the cabin.

'Found anything interesting?' she asked.

'What's it to you?'

'Oh nothing,' Mazy sat down on the bench that ran around the side of the cabin. 'There's something I wanted to ask you.'

Blind Lightning Henry pushed the papers to one side, looked at his niece and screwed up his eyes to peer at her. 'Well?'

'How do you divide up the treasure if you find some?'

Her uncle pushed back his chair, 'If we find treasure? Well, normally half of it goes to the captain as he has to maintain the ship. The rest is divided up between the crew. Why do you ask? You found some have you?'

Mazy pushed her hand into her pocket and pulled out the small, dirty brown bag she had found under the bench she was now sitting on. She had already looked inside it and she knew it contained coins and there was something else. Mazy tipped out the coins onto the table in front of her uncle but hidden from him she also took out a small silver locket and held it in her clenched fist.

Her uncle leant forward, his eyes wide open as he stared at the pile of coins. He pushed them around with a finger mentally counting them up. 'That's a pretty good amount of treasure you've found there. Where did you find it?'

'Here, on The Scarlet Arrow, under this bench.'

Her uncle tilted his head to one side, 'Was that all?'

'There was something else.'

'A treasure map?'

A treasure map, thought Mazy, why would he suggest a treasure map? She had found one but she wasn't going to tell him. There was a nagging feeling at the back of her mind. Maybe one day she would come back to the island and search for the treasure herself.

'No, no treasure map.'

'Then what?'

Mazy unclenched her fist and held out the small silver locket. She saw her uncle's eyes go wide. He leant forward towards her and tried to snatch the locket from her hand. She quickly pulled back away from him and hid the locket under the table.

'That's not yours,' he said hoarsely.

Mazy shuffled sideways along the bench away from her uncle who was staring hard at her. 'It's not yours either,' she said stuffing her hand into her pocket.

'What is it *you* want, Mazy?'

'Answers.'

Her uncle sat back and smiled. 'Answers is it. And if I give you the answers will you give me the locket?'

'Maybe.'

Her uncle folded his arms, said nothing and looked at Mazy.

'Whose ship is this?' Mazy began.

''Tis ours now, or mine being that I'm the Captain.'

'Someone told me that The Black Booger was once The Scarlett Arrow.'

'Well as you can see that is a lie given that The Black Booger is now at the bottom of the ocean.'

Mazy fiddled with the locket in her pocket. Her uncle wasn't going to give her the answers that easily. 'Why did you have a table in The Black Booger with Jehoshaphat the Terrible's name on it?'

'Won it fair and square in a fight. That's where I nearly lost both my legs. They was a fearsome bunch of cutthroat pirates. Thought they could take my ship. We fought them for days, no, weeks or even months.'

Blind Lightning Henry was waving his arms around and speaking faster and faster as he told the story of his fight with the fearsome Jehoshaphat the Terrible and how in the end he stole the table. He ended, 'That Jehoshaphat thought she could get the better of me but we were victorious. Last we seen of them was sailing away with broken masts and sails. Kept the table as a trophy.'

Mazy stared at her uncle. There was dead silence in that little cabin. The ship rocked as it was gently pulled along by the wind. Mazy took out the locket from inside her pocket and pressed the catch to open it as her uncle tried to take it from her again. She pulled back from his grabbing hand and looked inside. She saw two small painted pictures. One was of a young woman with red hair wearing a polka dot scarf over her head. On her shoulder was a parrot. In the other half of the locket was a picture of a young man. He was wearing a black three-pointed hat and in the background was a sailing ship. It was a picture of her uncle when he was a young man.

'You said she, uncle. Jehoshaphat was a woman.'

Her uncle slumped back in his seat. Gone was Blind Lightning Henry. Gone was the Uncle full of exciting tales. Mazy thought he looked like a small crumpled collection of clothing. Eventually he whispered, 'Aye, she was.'

'Were you in love with her?' she asked quietly.

'Indeed I was. You see Mazy, Jehoshaphat The Terrible was my wife.'

The cabin remained quiet. Mazy waited watching her uncle. He looked so sad she thought.

'What happened, uncle,' she asked gently.

'I'll tell you Mazy but it's not a story I'd like you to repeat to anyone. You promise that and I'll tell you the whole story and then you will give me that locket.'

'I promise,' said Mazy.

So her uncle told her of how he and Jehoshaphat sailed together in The Black Booger with the crew he had now. They had enjoyed adventures and long trips at sea. It was she who had obtained the parrot and named it 'Left a Bit'. Then one day she came to him to tell of a treasure map, and an island and a giant. She had been offered a ship of her own if she went to recover the treasure. He warned her against it. He said it would be too dangerous but she was determined. She said if he wouldn't go with her she would go on her own. And one night, under the cover of darkness, she sailed out of Charlestown Harbour in The Scarlet Arrow and was never seen again.

'After that, I swore I wouldn't let another woman sail with me. It wasn't they brought bad luck. I couldn't bear to lose anyone that dear to me again.'

Mazy thought about where they had found The Scarlet
Arrow and shivered at what may have happened to
Jehoshaphat and her crew. She closed the locket and
handed it to her uncle. He looked so old she thought. 'I
won't tell anyone,' she said.

'No you won't,' he replied pocketing the locket. 'Now
go and get some sleep. Long way to go before we get
home.'

In the end, The Scarlet Arrow made good time. The
crew had managed to stitch up some more of the tatty
sails and the wind blew stronger and stronger driving
the ship towards home. The Scarlet Arrow sailed into
the port late one afternoon. The captain had divided up
the coins that Mazy had found so the crew were happy
to be home and with some money to spend. Mazy
walked down the gangplank followed by Melwyn and

Jory.

'Look,' said Melwyn, 'There's Mr Borlaise with your black cat.'

Mazy said, 'FeeBe,' at the same time Jory said, 'Storm.' And they both laughed.

'Ok,' said Jory, 'FeeBe.'

'Hello Mr Borlaise,' said Mazy picking up FeeBe. The cat purred loudly and snuggled into her arms.

'Hello ladies,' replied Mr Borlaise from under his bushy eyebrows. 'Told your parents you'd be away for a few days but I daresay they'll be glad to see you back. How goes it captain,' he continued as they were joined by Mazy's uncle, 'see you come back with a different ship.'

'Lost the other one in a fight with a giant,' boomed the

captain.

'Three giants,' corrected Mazy, grinning up at him.

'That's right,' he agreed quickly, 'three giants and a giant squid. And if it wasn't for these three youngsters we'd be all gone the way of The Black Booger. Bravest crew I've ever sailed with.' Blind Lightning Henry gave Mazy, Melwyn and Jory a big smile and headed off towards The Crab and Crossed Claws.

'Looks like he got his sight back an all,' smiled Mr Borlaise watching the captain walk away from him.

'Maybe he did,' agreed Mazy. 'Come on Melwyn, let's go home.'

The two girls headed up the path away from the port. Jory watched them go and sighed before he too turned towards The Crab and Crossed Claws.

'What are you going to do with your share of the money Melwyn?' asked Mazy as they walked along side by side.

'Give it to me mum, I suppose.'

'You could use some to go on to be a Doctor like you want to. Then you could be the ship's doctor.'

'Huh,' grunted Melwyn. 'I wasn't planning to go to sea again ever, ever, again, thank you very much.'

Mazy laughed. 'Oh I am,' she said and remembered the treasure map still in her pocket. 'I want to go as soon as I can. But I'm going to give my share to my mum and dad so my dad doesn't have to work so hard and mum can have some new clothes and maybe we won't have to eat potatoes all the time.'

They came to the lane that led away to Mazy's house.

'See you at school tomorrow?' said Melwyn.

'Oh gosh,' exclaimed Mazy. 'School. Mrs. Scroggin. I suppose so.'

'See you tomorrow Crazy Mazy.'

'See you tomorrow, Smellie Mellie and thanks for coming back to rescue us.'

Mazy watched her friend walk away and then she turned towards her home and food and bed but at the same time started to think of ways she could avoid Ralph the Wrath and come back with huge amounts of treasure next time.

Charlestown Harbour.

Charlestown Harbour lies on the south coast of Cornwall, England and is the only remaining example of an 18th century port. It started life as a small fishing village named West Polmear. The village changed considerably when a port was constructed between 1791 and 1801. At this time it was used primarily for the export of copper.

In later years the port prospered from the export of locally sourced china clay. However, the port was unable to take ships of any real size and its last commercial shipment of china clay departed in year 2000. Since that date it has become a popular tourist attraction. Its unique location and collection of a small fleet of tall ships has drawn film crews from around the world. Today it is a UNESCO world heritage site.

Giants of Cornwall.

There are many myths and legends about a number of giants who lived in Cornwall. The most well known are probably the husband and wife, Cormoran and Cormelian. They are famously responsible for building the iconic St. Michaels Mount. There was also Trecobben who was friends of Cormoran. There was also The Giant of Carn Galver and a giant named Bedruthan.

The giant in my story, Ralph the Wrath, lived in a cave on the north coast of Cornwall, and called Ralph's Cupboard. He was known to prey on passing ships and steal their treasure and kill the crew. He was also reputed to throw huge boulders to sink ships. These boulders still lie where they fell and can be seen at low tide.

About the author.

 Peter has lived in Cornwall for more than 40 years. Following a career with the Devon and Cornwall Constabulary he took up writing children's stories in his retirement. He is a member of The St Austell Society of Artists. He has painted many scenes of Charlestown Harbour and the tall ships that are moored there. His work is for sale at The Charlestown Gallery.

Also by the same author.

Timmy in a box.

Timberley Three and the secret of Linden Hall.

Slugina.

Tales from the Gooshwan Valley.

theauthorpeterp@gmail.com